MURDER

IN

GEORGETOWN

An Eleanor Roosevelt Mystery

Elliott Roosevelt

Thomas Dunne Books / St. Martin's Minotaur

New York

A THOMAS DUNNE BOOK.
An imprint of St. Martin's Press.

MURDER IN GEORGETOWN. Copyright © 1999 by Gretchen Roosevelt, Ford
Roosevelt, and Jay Wahlin, as trustees under the trust instrument of the
"26 Trust". All rights reserved. Printed in the United States of America.
No part of this book may be used or reproduced in any manner whatso-
ever without written permission except in the case of brief quotations
embodied in critical articles or reviews. For information, address St. Martin's Press, 175 Fifth Avenue, New York, N.Y. 10010.

Library of Congress Cataloging-in-Publication Data

Roosevelt, Elliott.
        Murder in Georgetown :   an Eleanor Roosevelt mystery / Elliott
Roosevelt. — 1st ed.
            p.   cm.
        "A Thomas Dunne book"
        ISBN 0-312-24221-2
        1. Roosevelt. Eleanor, 1884–1962 Fiction.   I. Title.
PS3535.0549M84   1999   99–26719
813'.54—dc21   CIP

First St. Martin's Minotaur Edition: October 1999

10   9   8   7   6   5   4   3   2   1

MURDER

IN

GEORGETOWN

I

FOR FRANKLIN D. ROOSEVELT, President of the United States, Wednesday, February 13, 1935, began as nearly every other day began: sitting in his bed propped up by fat pillows, eating breakfast from his tray and scanning the morning newspapers. A Camel cigarette lay at hand, already in its holder, ready to be lighted as his first of the day as soon as he had finished eating and was drinking his coffee.

Marguerite "Missy" LeHand, his longtime personal secretary, sat on the side of the bed, near the foot, eating from her own tray. She wore a sheer white peignoir over a dark-blue silk nightgown. She, too, was scanning newspapers, occasionally marking a story or editorial with red ink to bring it to the President's attention.

This was their morning routine. Newspapers from as far north as Boston, as far south as Atlanta, and as far west as Pittsburgh arrived by train before dawn

and were delivered to the White House for the President's attention. Lately newspapers from Cleveland, Chicago, Louisville, and St. Louis had been coming in irregularly by airplane.

"My God!" said Missy. "Sargent Peavy is dead. Somebody murdered him! And . . . Jessica Dee . . . Isn't Jessica Dee the girl Mrs. R sent up to the Hill to work for the Kingfish?"

"Louie did that, actually," said the President. "But I believe that's the name. Jessica Dee. Is she dead, too?"

"No. She's in jail. Charged with murder. She's accused of murdering Sargent Peavy!"

"Let me see," the President said, reaching for the paper.

The story—

PEAVY OF FED MURDERED

LONG'S STAFF MEMBER ACCUSED

Sargent Peavy, member of the Board of Governors of the Federal Reserve System, was murdered last evening in his home in Georgetown.

Jessica Dee, a member of the Capitol Hill staff of Senator Huey Long, has been arrested and accused of the crime.

D.C. police headquarters received a telephone call at about 8:00 P.M. from a woman described

as hysterical who screamed that Mr. Peavy had been murdered in his home and then hung up. When police arrived at the address, they found the lights burning and the doors locked. They decided to break in, but before they could do so a car driven by Mrs. Letitia Peavy pulled into the driveway. She admitted the officers with her key, and inside the house, in the main bedroom, they found the body of Sargent Peavy, killed by a single bullet fired into his forehead.

The body, police say, was completely nude.

Mrs. Peavy immediately accused Jessica Dee of the murder of her husband. Other evidence shortly discovered led police to accept the accusation and send officers to arrest Miss Dee.

The D.C. police department has refused to say what that other evidence was.

Miss Dee was arrested at her home and taken to the District jail, where she was formally charged with murder and held for a court appearance likely to take place today.

DISTINGUISHED PROFESSORS

Sargent Peavy, who was appointed to the Federal Reserve Board by President Roosevelt in 1933, was formerly a professor of economics at Harvard. Regarded as a distinguished economist, he served also as a member of the boards of directors of several banks.

He was forty-four years old.

Mrs. Letitia Peavy, née Craft, was married to Sargent Peavy in 1919. She, too, was a member of the Harvard faculty, a professor of political science. When Peavy accepted appointment to the Federal Reserve and the couple moved to Washington, she became a professor of political science at George Washington University.

The couple had no children, and Mr. Peavy is survived by his wife, his father, a brother, and a sister.

THE ACCUSED

Jessica Dee is a subject of the British monarchy, having come to this country from Edinburgh, Scotland. She is twenty-six years old.

For about two years she served as a receptionist and law librarian at the firm of Covington & Burling. In recent months she has been employed by Senator Huey Long of Louisiana, as a general administrative assistant.

Senator Long was not available for a comment.

Lieutenant Edward Kennelly, homicide detective, said that Miss Dee has not cooperated with the police in their investigation, but that he has enough evidence in hand to justify the charge of murder.

At approximately the same time when the President was reading the story of the murder, Mrs. Roosevelt returned to the White House from a morning horseback ride in Rock Creek Park. She was fifty-one years old that year. Americans who had not seen her in person generally did not realize that their First Lady was almost six feet tall. She had something of a perverse talent for choosing clothes that did not flatter her—hats in particular—but her riding clothes suited her perfectly, and with them she wore her hair tied back by a wide band of yellow silk. As she strode through the halls of the White House, gently slapping her boots with her riding crop, she was a stunning, appealing figure.

She was scheduled to meet for breakfast with a delegation of congressional wives who wanted her to win the President's support for an appropriation to study the extent and effect of geophagy in the South. Hundreds of thousands of people, it had been reported, supplemented their meager diets by eating clayey soil, from which they obtained bulk and minerals. Mrs. Roosevelt had been shocked to hear it and wanted to know more.

She had only ten minutes to change out of her riding clothes and dress for the breakfast. Even so she took time to stop in her study to see if there were any urgent messages for her.

Malvina "Tommy" Thompson had found the same

story that Missy LeHand found for the President.

"Oh, dear! Please telephone Lieutenant Kennelly and ask him if he can see me at, say, ten-thirty. I'll come to his office. I would like to interview poor Jessica."

Mrs. Roosevelt's mind went back to a day in October of 1934 when she first heard the name Jessica Dee. She heard it from Louis McHenry Howe.

It was probably not too strong a statement to say that Franklin Roosevelt would not have been President of the United States if it had not been for the man he called Louie. Louis Howe was Roosevelt's backroom manipulator and string-puller. They had met in Albany when FDR was a first-term state senator. The young Roosevelt had been a powerful personality and orator but naive about politics, about how things got done, how a man got what he wanted. Howe was a small, chain-smoking gnome who couldn't make any kind of speech, but he had been a newspaperman, a political reporter, and he knew the ins and outs of politics. The two men made a formidable team. When the time came, it had been Howe who had dragged FDR out of the despondency and lethargy that had overcome him when he had to face the reality that he would never walk again. Howe had persuaded him to run for governor, to make the Al Smith nominating speech, and to run for President.

At first Mrs. Roosevelt had disliked him intensely. Then he had become her mentor. No one could remain politically naive with Louis McHenry Howe around.

On that morning in October, five months ago Howe had recruited Mrs. Roosevelt to help him with a little political scheme he had in mind.

"We've got to figure that quiet, modest, self-effacing man the Kingfish is going to run for President against Frank in 1936," he had said. "If that were all he might have in mind, I wouldn't worry about him, but Huey Long is one of the most dangerous men in America. He may be thinking of starting his own political party. He may be thinking of challenging Frank at the convention. We can't know what he has in mind."

"Well, Louie, I'm not sure what we can do about it."

Howe was one of the few political people around the President that Mrs. Roosevelt called by his first name, even by his nickname, Louie. He was a small, untidy man whose suits fit him ill. Dandruff flakes lay on his shoulders, cigarette ash on his lapels and vest. In the course of a day he would smoke five or six packs of his signature brand of cigarettes, Sweet Caporals. He was always wreathed in smoke and he hacked constantly.

"I have an idea," he said. "I'd like to send a girl up to the Hill, to see if she can't get a job working for the

Kingfish. Really, she'll be working for us."

"Is that ethical?" Mrs. Roosevelt asked with a sly, measured smile.

"Of course it's not ethical," said Howe. "But all's fair in love and war . . . and politics. Think about it. The Kingfish could hurt Frank's candidacy in 1936. Suppose he split the Democrats and brought the Republicans back in."

"Or worse," said Mrs. Roosevelt, "suppose he were elected."

"Exactly."

"But really, Louie, how can we place a girl on his staff? Whatever Senator Long is, he is no fool."

Howe grinned. "Yes, he is. Wait till you meet the girl. You'll see what I mean. Her name is Jessica Dee, and Jessica could melt Billy Sunday. If she goes to the Kingfish with a letter of recommendation from you—"

"But I have another ethical concern. Won't we be throwing the poor young woman to the lions?"

"I want you to meet her. I think you'll agree that Jessica is quite capable of taking care of herself."

"What does she do now? I mean, is she employed somewhere?"

"Indeed she is. She works for the law firm of Covington and Burling, as a receptionist and law librarian."

"How did she come to your attention?"

"Believe it or not, through Justice Oliver Wendell Holmes. He met her somewhere, was impressed by her, and invited her to his home. As I think you know, the justice asks a few young people to come to his home and read to him. Jessica did that, and he brought her to the attention of Justice Brandeis, who in turn brought her to the attention of Dean Acheson. And so she wound up being employed at Acheson's firm. It was Acheson who introduced her to me."

"Well . . . I will meet her."

"You will be pleasantly surprised."

Mrs. Roosevelt had invited Jessica to the White House for lunch and had seen immediately what Howe had meant when he said the young woman could melt—by which he had undoubtedly meant entice— Billy Sunday. She was a diminutive, exceptionally attractive young woman of twenty-six. Blond, with a modest though shapely figure, she possessed an ingenuous outgoing charm that appealed to Mrs. Roosevelt. It was easy to see that men would find her irresistable.

She was modestly and stylishly dressed in a black calf-length skirt cinched by a wide black patent-leather belt, a black jacket, and a white blouse.

The way she spoke English would also win over anyone. "Ah, Mrs. Rrrroosevelt," she said. " 'Tis most honored I am to meet ye."

"Where are you from, Jessica?"

"Edinburrrough."

"How long have you been in the States?"

Jessica laughed lightly. "Long enow to ha' un-learned me Scots burrr. But . . . it has proved useful. Some people like it."

"Yes. It is charming."

" 'Tis no natural," said Jessica. "I learned it. I will take you into my confidence, Ma'am, as I did Mr. Justice Holmes. I'm nayy Scot. Noo. I am a Polish Jew."

Mrs. Roosevelt frowned. "*Indeed!*"

"Aye. We hear much these days about German anti-Semitism. The most virulent anti-Semitism in the world is Polish. I am a child of a Jewish family from Lublin. My real name is Lala Berg. When Poland became a nation in 1919, it— Well. Let me explain. My family lived in Lublin, but not one of us could speak a word of Polish. We spoke Hebrew. Some Yiddish. But what we spoke on the streets and to our neighbors was Russian. The Russians, after all, had ruled in that part of Poland for many, many years. Why speak Polish? Why not speak the language of the governors, the masters? Well . . . The Poles resented it. Anyway, our family was most fortunate. A Zionist organization committed itself to rescuing Jewish children from the pogrom they expected in Poland. When I was ten years old, I was sent to Edinburgh. I was adopted by a Scots family. They named me Dee, after the river. I have never seen my Jewish family since."

"That is tragic, child," said Mrs. Roosevelt, all but tearful.

"I was one of the few lucky ones. Mr. Justice Holmes taught me American history. I taught him Hebrew. Can you imagine? At his age he wanted to learn Hebrew, so he could read early texts of the Bible and compare them with the translations with which he was familiar."

"How did you come to meet Mr. Justice Holmes?"

"Luck," said Jessica. "The dear old man was always attentive to girls he found attractive. I was a delivery girl, which was all the work I could get in 1930. I made a delivery to his home from time to time. One night he came to the door himself. He invited me to come into his home and visit with him. At first I just read to him, which he loved to have young people do because his eyesight was failing. Then he learned I could read and speak Hebrew, and the next time I saw him he had a Hebrew book. He asked me to read it to him, and translate. Would you believe it? He became a little bit fluent. But . . . I hear he is very low, now."

"His health is failing rapidly," said Mrs. Roosevelt sadly.

They talked for an hour. Mrs. Roosevelt gave Jessica a letter of introduction to Senator Huey Long—

Dear Senator Long,
The bearer of this letter is my new young friend

Jessica Dee who is looking for employment in a congressional office. I thought you might be interested in interviewing her.

I will leave it to her to fill you in about her curriculum vitae. As you will learn, she is not an American citizen and is anxious to work in government, where she can learn more about our country. She is at present employed with Covington & Burling. She was brought to my attention by Mr. Louis Howe, who learned of her indirectly from Mr. Justice Holmes.

If you can spare the time to give her a hearing, I will regard it as a courtesy to me.

Sincerely yours,
Eleanor Roosevelt

"My dear," she had said to Jessica, "you must understand that Senator Long is a most erratic man. If he gives you any trouble, let me know. I will not leave you without employment."

Somewhat to Mrs. Roosevelt's surprise, Senator Long had hired Jessica immediately. Shortly she received a handwritten note from the senator—

Dear Eleanor,
All kinds of thanks for sending me Jessica. She is a delight. If there is anything I can do for you, please let me know.

Huey

She wondered if Howe had not done something more to encourage him. She tried not to think about the possibility that Jessica herself had done something to encourage him.

From time to time over the ensuing months, Jessica had come to the White House, invariably in the evening. She was reporting to Howe what she overheard in the senator's office. Two or three times Mrs. Roosevelt saw her and invited her to share an evening pot of coffee. Jessica never said anything about the Kingfish, except that he was a funny man. Her reports to Howe were undoubtedly more specific.

When Mrs. Roosevelt returned to her study after her breakfast with the congressional wives, Tommy Thompson reported that Lieutenant Kennelly had said he would be honored to see her any time. She should call, and he would arrange for her to enter police headquarters unseen by the reporters who hung around the place. She dictated answers to eight letters and at 10:45 left for headquarters.

II

LIEUTENANT KENNELLY WELCOMED MRS. Roosevelt into his cluttered little office. She had visited him there several times before and had always been amused by the half dozen cups with dregs of coffee in them that sat on his scarred yellow-oak desk, rusty filing cabinet, and windowsill, as well as by the dead flies that lay on the windowsill and on the floor. He smoked Luckies, and a heap of butts always filled his big glass ashtray, sometimes smoldering from the fire in his active cigarette if it lay on the pile.

Kennelly was a bulky Irishman with a glowing flushed complexion and prematurely white hair. In a conversation months ago he had remarked it was the business of the Irish in America to enforce the law. She knew he had begun his police career as a beat patrolman and was proud of his occupation and the rank he had achieved in it.

He helped the First Lady take off her coat and her

fox neckpiece, and he hung them for her on his hall tree. She was wearing a gray knit dress.

"I find it almost impossible to believe that Miss Dee could be guilty of murder," said Mrs. Roosevelt.

"She's an appealing girl. But I've got a good deal of evidence against her."

"Have you indeed? If it's not entirely confidential, I would appreciate knowing what it is."

"It is somewhat confidential at present, but I know I can trust your discretion, Ma'am." He reached for a pack of cigarettes; but, probably because he remembered the First Lady did not like cigarette smoke, he put the pack down. "In the first place, Miss Dee and Professor Peavy were lovers. That is to say, they were until recently. She admits to the affair but says the professor told her he wanted to break it off. She says the affair was broken off about a month ago and that she wasn't in his house since about the middle of last month. She says he was having a new affair, with another woman, already—a spectacular redhead."

"Did Mrs. Peavy know about the affair with Miss Dee? Is that why she accused her?"

Kennelly nodded emphatically. "She says the affair threatened her marriage and also threatened the professor's position on the Federal Reserve Board. She says she told him he had to break it off, and she says he promised he would. She named two friends she said could confirm the affair and the promise to break off.

We called them, and they did confirm it. She figures Miss Dee killed him in a fit of rage when he told her he was breaking it off."

"Has an autopsy been performed?"

"Yes. Peavy died instantly, from a single shot fired into his head from a nine-millimeter automatic pistol."

"Did the autopsy show whether or not Mr. Peavy had engaged in sexual intimacy just before his death?"

The already-flushed face of Lieutenant Kennelly flushed a deeper red. "Yes, Ma'am," he said in a subdued voice. "He . . . uh . . . yes."

"In other words his seminal vesicles were all but empty," said Mrs. Roosevelt. "I am not unacquainted with such matters, Lieutenant."

Kennelly continued to blush. "Very well. He'd had sex immediately before he died."

"And Miss Dee?"

"When she was searched, she showed no obvious sign of having engaged in sex in the couple of hours before. On the other hand, she was only searched by jail matrons, not examined by a doctor."

"Well . . . Go ahead and smoke, Lieutenant. This is your office, not mine. So . . . What other evidence have you?"

Kennelly paused while he lit a Lucky. Then he reached into a drawer and pulled out a small white envelope. He opened the envelope and dumped an earring on the desk. "We found that on the bedroom floor,

not far from the body. Miss Dee admits it is hers."

Mrs. Roosevelt examined the earring. It was of white gold: a sapphire in a setting of tiny diamonds. "Rather expensive, I should think," she said.

"It was a gift from Professor Peavy. When Mrs. Peavy found out he had given Miss Dee such an expensive gift, that was when she decided he was in love with her and that the affair had to end. We asked Miss Dee to produce its mate. She claims it is missing, probably stolen from her apartment."

"I must say this, Lieutenant— This earring is for a pierced ear. It did not just clip on. An earring that clips on might well fall off; they often do. Earrings for pierced ears hardly ever fall off. Did you find the little nut that would have held it in place?"

"No, and we searched thoroughly."

"What other evidence do you have? Any?"

"A thorough forensic search includes removing the stoppers from the drains, to see what's in the traps. In the pipe under the bathtub we found long blond hair. Miss Dee has long blond hair. Mrs. Peavy does not. Mrs. Peavy says she knew Miss Dee was taking showers there, after having intimate relations with the professor."

"She does not deny she had such relations."

"Two more things," said Kennelly. "On the driveway outside the house we found a surgical glove. The

killer may have worn it. It would prevent leaving fingerprints—"

"But since everyone knows Miss Dee had been in
the house often, her fingerprints would be there, and
she would have no reason to—"

"There would be a more important reason for
wearing rubber gloves," said Kennelly. "When a person fires a handgun, a minute quantity of burned gunpowder is blasted against the skin of the hand. Some
of it penetrates. It can be discovered by coating the
hand with hot paraffin, which will lift the gunpowder
residue so it can be detected by applying an acid."

"What evidence links Miss Dee to the glove?"

"It has a slit in the third finger. That may have been
caused by an exceptionally long fingernail. Miss Dee
wears her fingernails long."

"I find that fanciful, Lieutenant Kennelly."

"I agree. But I have one more item, more important
than any of the others. When we went to arrest Miss
Dee last night, we found her at home, at about ten.
Naturally, I asked her where she had been all evening
and specifically at about eight o'clock. She said she
had been at home all evening except for twenty
minutes or so just before eight o'clock when she had
gone down to the neighborhood grocery store to buy
a quart of milk. But she hadn't been to the store. The
proprietor says he knows her and she was not in his
store all evening. When I confronted her with that, she

just clammed up. She said he was wrong."

Mrs. Roosevelt shook her head. "That doesn't look good, does it?"

"It looks good to *me*. I'm trying to close a murder case."

"May I talk with her?"

"Yes. Since it's you."

"Alone?"

"Since it's you, Ma'am."

Kennelly left and let Mrs. Roosevelt meet with Jessica in his office.

Because she was charged with murder and was outside the bars of the jail, a matron handcuffed Jessica to the chair by her left wrist. For the first minute of their meeting, the girl's eyes switched back and forth from the First Lady to the cuff on her wrist. Mrs. Roosevelt thought the handcuff looked terribly big and heavy to be locked on the wrist of a slight young woman. Jessica's drab and tattered gray dress, the jail uniform, was too big for her. She wore no makeup. Her face was puffy, maybe from want of sleep, maybe from crying.

" 'Tis kind of ye to come to see me," Jessica said softly. "They want to put th' noose around me neck, y'noo."

"Their case is not all that strong," said Mrs. Roosevelt. "But you have *given* them the strongest evi-

dence they have against you. Sooner or later, before they do put that noose around your neck, you are going to have to tell where you were when you said you had stayed home all evening except for a visit to the grocery store."

"That was the wrrong thing to say. I could just have said that I was at home all evening. But— But two of me neighbors, a man and his wife, saw me going oot. I had to cover *that* somehoo."

"I surmise . . . Jessica . . . that you went out to spend some time with another man."

Jessica nodded. For a moment she stared at her chained wrist. "Aye . . ." she murmured. "But I canna tell ye who."

"You *must* tell who!"

Jessica shook her head. "If it comes to it . . . If it really comes down to it that I am going to the gallows, he will come forward and say who he is. He will save me."

"You have a great deal of confidence in someone," Mrs. Roosevelt said dryly.

"He is a fine gentleman. More prominent than poor Sargie was. A great deal richer. For noo I will place my trust in him."

"I hope you place it well, Jessica," Mrs. Roosevelt said solemnly.

· · ·

"Even so," Mrs. Roosevelt said to Kennelly after she told him Jessica would not identify her alibi witness, "I see critical weaknesses in your case."

"So do I," said Kennelly. "But tell me which ones *you* see."

"Apart from the fact that that kind of earring would not just *fall* off, apart from the fact that finding it on the floor within a few feet of the body is just too nice a coincidence—"

"Apart from that."

"Suppose she did shoot Mr. Peavy. Why would she then pick up the telephone and scream that he was dead? Wasn't it in *her* interest to let as much time elapse as possible, before the police came?"

Kennelly nodded. "I thought of that. I've also considered the possibility that Mrs. Peavy shot the professor. If so, why would *she* call the police? Are we to believe she killed her husband, then left the house and called the police, then came back just in time to see the police arrive?"

Mrs. Roosevelt smiled faintly. "I have observed before, Lieutenant Kennelly, that our minds work in very similar ways. So let me ask you a question. From what distance was Mr. Peavy shot?"

"I take your point," said Kennelly. "You want to know if there were powder burns on his forehead, if he was shot from close range. The answer is no. He was shot from . . . four or five feet away, at least."

"Meaning that his killer was a steady hand and something of a marksman. I cannot believe that Jessica Dee could coldly aim a pistol at her lover's forehead and shoot him dead with a bullet placed squarely in the middle of his forehead."

"It was a woman," said Kennelly.

"How do you know that?"

"Why was the professor stark, starin' naked—him a man who had just emptied his seminal vesicles?"

Mrs. Roosevelt raised her chin. "He could have emptied them into several women, Lieutenant. Jessica, certainly. Mrs. Peavy, of course. And since we know he had an affair with Jessica while married to Mrs. Peavy, the possibility there was another woman cannot be overlooked. Indeed, Jessica says he was seeing yet another woman: 'a spectacular redhead.' "

Kennelly turned down the corners of his mouth and nodded. "Our inquiry has developed some suggestion that there were other women. For example, the long blond hair was not the only long hair found in the drain. We also found some curly dark-brown hair."

"Then why Jessica?"

"She is the only one who has lied to us . . . and the only one we have in custody."

Her schedule for the day included a meeting with the six-year-old Shirley Temple, with whom she was to be photographed. The session was scheduled for the

Rose Garden, but someone had forgotten there were no roses in bloom in Washington in February. Anyway, by 12:30, when she was to meet the endearing tyke before the cameras, a mixture of rain and snow was falling on the sere garden. She met Shirley Temple in the East Room.

The little girl *was* endearing. *"My!"* she said. "This is a very big house! You must have a very profitable business to make it possible."

The microphones caught every word. The cameras recorded the expressions.

"Actually, Shirley," said Mrs. Roosevelt, "this house is not just ours. It belongs to the people of the United States. To all the people."

"All . . . ? Me, too?"

Mrs. Roosevelt nodded. "You are one of the owners."

The little girl beckoned to Mrs. Roosevelt to put her ear down. "Oh, Mrs. Roosevelt," she whispered. "They told me not to ask to go to the bathroom here. But I need to. If it's my house too . . . ?"

The news people never guessed where the First Lady led the little girl when they slipped out of the East Room for five minutes. They only noticed that both of them were beaming when they returned.

The First Lady had very little free time. After her brief meeting with Shirley Temple she went to her study and

read mail while she ate one of the tuna-salad sandwiches favored by her chosen housekeeper, Henrietta
Nesbitt—so despised by the President, who complained often that he could not get a decent meal in
the White House.

It was a sore point and the subject of a brief mem-
orandum from Mrs. Nesbitt that very afternoon. Mrs.
Roosevelt and her housekeeper had to think about the
food budget, which fed the Secret Service and some
of the press corps as well as the First Family. They
could hardly tell the Congress, which set the budget,
that in the middle of a great depression they needed
more money to stock the pantry. In any event, Mrs.
Roosevelt cared little about fancy food. She had once
told a reporter that she could feed her husband scrambled eggs five nights in succession and he wouldn't
notice. Nothing however could have been further from
the truth. The President looked forward to dinners
away from the White House, where he could have
what he called "a decent meal."

The food served there was not the only problem
with the White House. The whole building was in
shabby condition—state rooms, working offices, private quarters. It would have been difficult to say
whether neglect or clumsy restorations had done the
White House more harm. Nearly all of it was thread-
bare, with peeling paint and cracked plaster all too
evident. Besides the general surface decay, it was ap-

parent too that the structure was weak. Floors creaked. Walls shook. The President did not feel he could, in the midst of a great depression, go to the Congress and ask for a major appropriation to repair and redecorate the house. That would have to wait for some other president.

Lieutenant Kennelly called.

"Interesting news," he said. "Miss Dee has been released on bail."

"Isn't that unusual in a murder case?"

"Yes, Ma'am, very unusual. But she had a first-class lawyer, no less than Dean Acheson. He convinced the magistrate that she is not a dangerous person and not likely to scram. The magistrate set her bond at $10,000—figuring, I suppose, that she couldn't begin to raise that kind of money—and Acheson took the money out of his briefcase, in cash, and left here with his client in tow."

"That is a very great deal of money," Mrs. Roosevelt agreed. "She told me her new gentleman friend is wealthy. Apparently he *is*."

"Right. So there we have it."

"I remain unable to believe, Lieutenant, that Jessica could have committed the murder. I hope you mean to continue the investigation."

"I do, Ma'am. I very definitely do."

"Please keep me informed. I shall do all I can to

help solve the mystery—or, as I should now say, mysteries."

"Mysteries?"

"Yes, Lieutenant Kennelly, *two* mysteries. Who killed Mr. Sargent Peavy and who is Jessica's wealthy paramour. The two questions may be intimately linked."

III

THE PRESIDENT WAS NOT a patient man. When he sent to Congress a piece of legislation he considered vital, he expected Congress to act on it promptly. It had done so in the first week of his administration. It had done so in the famous Hundred Days. But now—

"Louie, how do we light a fire under those men?"

They sat in the Oval Office, the President behind his desk. He had slipped off his wooden wheelchair and into his comfortably upholstered armchair. He kept his feet propped up on a little platform under his desk. He wore a gray three-piece suit this morning. His watch rested in the pocket of his jacket, secured by a watch chain hooked into the buttonhole of his lapel. He had a Camel alight in a long holder.

"We can't," Louis Howe said simply. "Congress is feeling its oats. A lot of senators and representatives feel they abdicated their powers and responsibilities when they went along with so much of your program,

so now they are going to take their good old time."

"A lot of them owe their seats to this administration."

"Not a majority. And not the leadership."

"Louie, we've *got* to get Social Security. We've *got* to get the WPA."

Howe shook out a Sweet Caporal and lit it from the fire in the butt of the one he had smoked down to a stub. "Frank, it's going to take some doing," he said.

"We may have lost a senator yesterday," said the President. "I mean the Kingfish. I asked Babs to show me the letter she sent him, asking him to do something for that young woman Jessica Dee. I can imagine how he feels about it now, she having been charged with murder."

"Putting Jessica in the Kingfish's office was a stroke of genius, if you don't mind me tooting my own horn," said Howe.

The President laughed. "Well, you know what John L. Lewis says. 'He who tooteth not his own horn, the same shall not be tooted.' But the Kingfish may be mad at us now."

"He literally doted on her until she was arrested for murder. If you met her, you'd see why."

"She was supposed to be a spy," said the President. "Did she learn anything worth knowing?"

Howe grinned. "The Kingfish made a comment on your social legislation, Social Security and the rest of

it. He said you had just figured out what *he* had known since he was a boy. He said you had just now learned what you should have learned when you were in knee pants."

"That sounds as if he'll support the legislation—if he hasn't changed his mind because we sent an accused murderer to work for him. I wish we hadn't done that, Louie."

Mrs. Roosevelt had been asked to write a daily newspaper column, and this morning she decided to try it, just to see if she could do it. She realized that her schedule would not allow her to write one column each day, so she would have to write several, perhaps a week's worth, in one session. She dictated to Tommy.

The first, experimental column, which she knew she would not send to the newspaper syndicate, was on the subject of partisanship—

It is strange to me how much partisanship influences otherwise objective men and women. Last month I sat in the gallery of the House of Representatives and listened to the President deliver his State of the Union message. Some of his statements were quite commonplace, platitudes indeed, about the need to restore prosperity, to reduce unemployment, etc. When he said some

of these self-evident things, the Democrats on the floor burst into wild applause, as though they had never heard such brilliant and original ideas. The Republicans, hearing the same unexceptional ideas, sat in glum silence, staring at their feet. I believe he could have read the Declaration of Independence and got the same reaction from both sides of the aisle.

She finished that column and had begun to dictate another when the telephone rang. Tommy answered and asked if Mrs. Roosevelt wanted to speak to Jessica Dee.

"I'm just calling," Jessica said—somewhat breathlessly, the First Lady thought . . . "to tell you how very much I appreciate your kindness in coming to see me when I was in jail."

"It's good of you to call. I'd like to see you. Could you come by the White House?"

"Certainly. Whenever it is convenient for you."

"I have no luncheon scheduled," said Mrs. Roosevelt. "Come at twelve-thirty if you can."

Mrs. Nesbitt sent up lunch: a macaroni salad served with celery and carrot sticks, also coffee and an assortment of small pastries.

"How does Senator Long react to your being charged with a serious crime?" Mrs. Roosevelt asked

Jessica as soon as they were seated at the card table on which lunch was served.

"He's a dear mon," said Jessica. "He told me I could stay on the job as long as I could stay out of jail. When I told him I was coming to see you, he sent his best wishes."

"Do you want to tell me what happened between you and Mr. Peavy? I mean, what sort of relationship did you have? Can you explain why long blond hair was found in the bath drain in the Peavy home?"

"My lawyer, Mr. Acheson, has given me firm instructions to talk to nobody. But . . . I trust *you*, Mrs. Rrrosevelt. I'm not ashamed of what I've done. I suppose my hair was found in the drain because Sargie and I used to take showers together. He loved to take showers with me. He'd wash me, and I'd wash him."

"You didn't kill him."

"Noo. But I'm not ashamed of what I did do. I had a love affair with Sargie, for about six months. I had others before him. And I'm havin' another one noo. Men find me attractive. And I like men. I like things like taking a shower with a man."

"Mr. Peavy was a married man," Mrs. Roosevelt said a little censoriously.

"As I often reminded him," said Jessica. She shrugged. "Letitia knew all about it. At fairst she did not object."

"She did not object?"

"I wasn't the fairst woman he had an affair with. Nor the second or third, either. Did you know Sargie? He was a most appealing man. He was . . . What is the word?"

"Charismatic."

"Yes. Charismatic. Handsome and funny. He always knew just what to say . . . a kind, thoughtful man."

"But how was it that Mrs. Peavy did not object to his having an affair?"

"I can only tell you what Sargie told me. He said he and Letitia were married by accident, as ye might say. His marriage itself was the result of a dalliance. You see, 'e got 'er with child. They married. She suffered a miscarriage. And there they were, noo bairn an' each married to a partner they didn't want. Shortly, he was trifling with another woman, and she was trifling with another man. He said a divorce would have been scandalous and an impediment to both their careers, as discreet dalliances would not be." Jessica paused and frowned. "Is that true? Isn't that an odd set of values?"

"It's a fact, my dear. It's an American attitude. A divorce would be very damaging to any man's career, in almost any field."

"And an affair wouldn't?"

"That would depend on the affair. It would depend mostly on discretion."

"He mentioned a woman he dallied with. Maybe you've heard of her: Clare Boothe, an editor at *Vanity Fair*. He laughed about it and said she'd moved on to bigger game: a Mr. Henry Luce. Maybe you've heard of *him*."

"I have indeed."

"I don't think he lied," Jessica said soberly.

"I suppose he didn't."

"Ahh . . . Anyway, Letitia has a friend . . . somewhere. A friend who's no doubt hoping the story won't come out."

"Yes . . ." said Mrs. Roosevelt. "And *you* have a friend who doesn't want his story to come out. He put up your bail."

"And he's paying my attorney."

"The name of that man is the key to your defense, Jessica. And you *need* a defense."

Whatever else Huey Long might have been, he was flamboyant. As he strode through the corridors of the White House, his wide-lapel-double-breasted jacket was unbuttoned and flapped around him. Curly hair hung over his flushed forehead. He might have been campaigning in a small town in Louisiana, since he stopped to shake the hand of everyone he encountered—all of them but with two or three exceptions members of the White House staff, most of them Negroes.

"Har y' there? I'm Huey Long. Glad t' meet ya."

To a uniformed butler he said, "By the Good Lord, this here is a beautiful house, ain't it? Mebbe live here myself someday. I'll remember you, son. I'll remember you."

He had come to see Mrs. Roosevelt, and she received him in her study on the second floor—in the same room where she'd had lunch with Jessica not long before.

"Har y', Eleanor? Doin' good, I hope. How's Frank?"

"We are both well, Senator. And how are you?"

"Fine as frog's hair," said the Kingfish. "Couldn't be better."

"Well, sit down, Senator. I had a little conversation with Jessica this morning. She's very grateful to you for keeping her in her job while this nasty business of the criminal charge is resolved."

Long sat down. He seemed relieved to do so and not be reminded he was not as tall as the First Lady. "That li'l girl," he said, "is as cute as any kitten I ever saw."

"May I ask you a very frank question, Senator?"

"You can ask me any question you like, Eleanor."

"Well . . . Someone put up a very great sum of money for Jessica's bond, to get her out of jail. I wondered if—?"

"If it was me? No, *Ma'am*. I'm a poor man, Eleanor.

I couldn't afford to do that, much as I'd like to've. It's Jessica, though, that I came to talk about."

"Oh?"

"I wondered if you'd seen this. Thursday afternoon edition. Ink's barely dry."

He handed her a folded newspaper, *The Washington Evening Star*. A two-column story below the center was about Jessica Dee—

ACCUSED PEAVY MURDERESS HAS POLICE RECORD

ONCE JAILED AS DELIVERY GIRL FOR BOOTLEGGER

Jessica Dee, accused of murdering Fed Board member Sargent Peavy, spent two days and nights in jail in 1931 after her arrest for being a runner for one of the city's most notorious bootleggers.

According to records of the now-defunct Prohibition Bureau, Miss Dee was arrested on Saturday, November 21, 1931, and was held in jail over the weekend until she was bailed out on Monday. The charge against her was that she was a delivery girl for Manfred "Manny" Schottenstein, a notoriously bold and successful bootlegger.

Schottenstein's customers would telephone

their orders, and the hooch they ordered would be delivered to their homes or businesses by one of the bootlegger's runners, some of whom were attractive young women. The booze was carried in purses, grocery bags, shopping bags, and sometimes in special pockets sewn into coats. Girls were favored for runners because they could look innocent.

Miss Dee was not, and is not now, a citizen of the United States. She is Scottish and a subject of His Majesty King George V.

She speaks with a distinctive Scotch burr which some customers found so charming that they specifically asked for her as their delivery girl.

Although paid well for her slightly risky errands, she earned additional money in the tips many customers saw fit to give her.

Bond was posted for her on Monday, November 23. As was customary in such cases, prohibition agents did not pursue the case further, and she was back at work that same evening.

The mug shots taken of her appear on page 3.

The mug shots did in fact appear, in three columns. Front-face, the young woman who was unquestionably Jessica Dee had a hard look she certainly did not show in person in 1935. A number board hung around her

neck, identifying her and showing the date of her arrest. The profile shot was full-length, showing that she was five-feet-three.

"I am sorry, Senator," said Mrs. Roosevelt. "I had no idea and would not have recommended her to you if I had."

"Oh, I don't mind, Eleanor," he said. "This will make good copy in Loo-siana. Th' ol' Kingfish has got him a first-class gal in his office. 'Improvement over the hookers he usually hires,' some will say."

"She certainly never told me about this aspect of her life."

"Didn't tell me, neither. But this does explain how she came to know Justice Oliver Wendell Holmes. The old boy bought his hooch from Manny, same as most everybody."

"I imagine she didn't tell Covington and Burling, either. And I wonder whom else she didn't tell."

The Kingfish chuckled. "Well, it makes her more interesting, not less."

Lieutenant Kennelly called. He had seen *The Evening Star*. "Explains something," he said. "She wasn't just the little law-firm receptionist, after all."

"She has been, for several years," said Mrs. Roosevelt.

"She kept her secret pretty well. It makes me wonder what other secrets she's got."

IV

MRS. ROOSEVELT HAD NEVER met Mrs. Letitia Peavy. Even so, she felt a social obligation to pay a call on the widow and express her condolences. Sargent Peavy had been a member of her husband's administration, in a sense—at least he had been a Roosevelt appointee—and the First Lady felt an obligation to pay a call and attend the funeral.

Somewhat to her surprise, she found Letitia Peavy alone in the home in Georgetown—alone, that is, except for the maid who took her coat and fur neckpiece. Teacups and a half-empty tray of cookies were evidence that Mrs. Roosevelt was not the first guest of the day. As she entered the living room and took the chair Letitia offered, she hoped someone else would appear while she was there.

"I was so terribly shocked to read of Mr. Peavy's death. Please accept my warmest sympathy."

"Thank you."

"I must confess that I know Miss Jessica Dee rather well."

"Not as well as you thought, I suspect," said Letitia wryly, nodding at *The Evening Star*, which lay on the coffee table.

"Indeed not. I hadn't the slightest suspicion."

Letitia Peavy, who was thirty-eight years old, was a compact woman with a taut, solid figure, except for her breasts, which were unfashionably large. She wore her mousy-brown hair marcelled like Jean Harlow's and used her lipstick in the bee-sting style popular in the twenties. She was dressed in mourning black.

"I am honored that you came, Mrs. Roosevelt."

"I regret that we meet only now, in these unhappy circumstances."

"Let me offer you tea," said Letitia.

"Thank you."

"I am not surprised by today's tabloid story," Letitia said as she poured tea from a large pot. "The girl told Professor Peavy all about it. Her story, of course, is that she was desperate, that she was eating from soup kitchens and sleeping on cold winter nights in jail cells that the police opened for the homeless."

"You knew about the relationship all along?"

"All along. Mrs. Roosevelt, Professor Peavy was not an entirely monogamous man. He was a something of a philanderer—though that word probably exag-

gerates." She shook her head. "Whatever he was, he was that even before we were married."

"You need not tell me."

Letitia sat stiffly, the corners of her mouth drawn down. "I would *like* to tell you. I've had no chance to talk with a sympathetic woman. You see, Mrs. Roosevelt, I was the professor's student. He taught at Harvard and, like many Harvard professors, taught a class at Radcliffe, where I was a student. I can't say he seduced me. I was ready, willing, and able to be seduced by my handsome professor. Well . . . Before long I was pregnant. If it had been discovered, he would have lost his position immediately. For a professor to have an affair with a student was not just against the rules; it was against the law. We kept it secret until I graduated. Two days after my graduation we married. We went to California for a wedding trip. I expected to have the baby there." She sighed. "Instead, I had a miscarriage."

"I'm sorry," murmured Mrs. Roosevelt.

"I'm not sure I was sorry. I'm not sure I wasn't relieved. By then I knew I wasn't the only student with whom . . . with whom he'd had a relationship. Well . . . Anyway, we were married, and that was that. I continued my education, earned a doctorate, and became a member of the Radcliffe faculty, later the Harvard faculty. He strayed from time to time. I knew he did. I set

my foot down on one thing. No more students. He could have ruined both our careers."

"I hear that one of his paramours was a rather prominent woman."

Letitia smiled. "Clare Boothe. She wears black underwear. Also, there was Amelia Earhart, briefly. She wears none."

Mrs. Roosevelt could not help but cover her mouth with her hand and join Letitia in a subdued little laugh.

"He usually told me about his women," Letitia continued. "They were no secret. Sometimes I was annoyed but rarely any more than annoyed. He always insisted he loved me and me alone, and I believe he spoke the truth about that. Except with Jessica. That was different. She really had her claws in him. He told me he was in love with her, which is something he never said about any of the others. That threatened my marriage. It threatened his position at the Fed, too. I laid down the law. He told her he was breaking off the affair, and she killed him."

Mrs. Roosevelt nodded sympathetically, paused and frowned, and then said, "There are reasons to think she didn't. I don't mean to defend her, but have you considered any other possibilities?"

"Not really. I think it's pretty obvious that she did it. How else would her earring have been found beside his body? Isn't that pretty conclusive evidence?"

"Was it you who identified the earring for the police?"

"Yes," said Letitia. "The professor showed them to me before he gave them to her. That was one of the rare occasions when I got angry. I reminded him that we could not afford expensive jewelry for ourselves, much less for him to give his mistress. That was when he told me he was in love with her."

"About when was that?" Mrs. Roosevelt asked.

"I can fix the date exactly. He wrote a check to pay for the earrings. It was dated January 10. He promised to tell her the earrings were a farewell present and that they had to break off the affair. I don't think he ever did tell her—that is, until Tuesday evening, when she killed him."

For a moment Letitia covered her eyes with a handkerchief that was lying on the coffee table.

"Jessica says she never saw Mr. Peavy after about the middle of January," Mrs. Roosevelt said quietly.

"If she wasn't in our bedroom Tuesday evening, then why was her earring lying beside his body? If they hadn't been in bed—in *my* bed—why was he stark naked?"

"Jessica says he was already seeing another woman."

"Of *course* she'd say that. She needs a mythical other woman to get herself off the hook."

"Suppose—just suppose, for the sake of analysis—

that he was seeing still another woman. Have you any idea who that might be?"

"I saw him eating lunch in a restaurant one day, with a rather good-looking young woman. I asked him later who she was, and he said she was a secretary at the Fed."

"Can you describe her?"

"She had one striking feature: long red hair."

"I see. Well . . . Where were you, Mrs. Peavy, at the time when Mr. Peavy was murdered?"

"Why do you ask?"

"I am assisting the police in a minor way," said Mrs. Roosevelt. "I have helped them investigate three other murders since I've been in the White House. My role, chiefly, is to preserve discretion and avoid scandal—that and to try to see that innocent people are not convicted. The police, in my experience, are apt to jump to conclusions. They like to settle cases. I agree that it looks very much as if Jessica Dee killed Mr. Peavy. But I would like to be *certain*."

Letitia nodded. "I, too, would like to be certain. I was in my car at the time, driving home from the university."

Back in the White House, Mrs. Roosevelt by chance encountered Stanlislaw Szczygiel, a senior agent of the Secret Service—whose name, fortunately, was pronounced *See*-gul. Sixty-three years old and on the

verge of retirement, Szczygiel had protected presidents since Grover Cleveland and knew the White House as intimately as any man alive. He was a squat, square man, both of face and physique, and perhaps his most memorable feature was his oversized, gin-reddened nose.

"Oh, Mr. Szczygiel, I am pleased to see you. I am sure you know about the tragic death of Mr. Sargent Peavy. I am trying to offer some assistance to the police, as you will remember I have done in one or two other cases, and I was wondering if the murder of the member of the Federal Reserve Board falls within the jurisdiction of the Secret Service. If so, perhaps you could help, too."

They stood in the second-floor hallway where Mrs. Roosevelt was on her way to her study.

"It does," said Szczygiel. "President Coolidge, by executive order, extended the jurisdiction of the Service to cabinet officers, some judges, and members of some important boards and commissions. We don't have nearly enough personnel to guard all those men, but we can try to meet threats to their lives. I suppose we could rationalize that if one member of the Board has been murdered, that is potentially a threat to the others. I mean, whatever motivated someone to murder one member might motivate the same person or persons to murder others." Szczygiel grinned. "Of course, I do understand that Mr. Peavy was probably

killed for personal motives not related to his official duties."

"A distinction we might temporarily overlook, might we not?" asked Mrs. Roosevelt with a sly smile in response to Szczygiel's grin.

"We might. We might indeed."

"Then I should be grateful if you could reserve a half hour or so to meet with me and Lieutenant Kennelly of the District police. Say, tomorrow morning?"

"Gladly, Ma'am."

Friday morning dawned fine and not too cold, a perfect day, the First Lady thought, for a canter in Rock Creek Park. Elinor Morgenthau joined her. Elinor was the wife of Henry Morgenthau, Secretary of the Treasury, and a Hudson Valley neighbor. The two women had been close friends for many years, and they often rode together. By a little after seven Mrs. Roosevelt was astride her horse Dot, riding in the brisk air less than half an hour after dawn. As always a military aide rode at a respectful distance behind.

"I believe you and Henry were friends of Sargent Peavy," said Mrs. Roosevelt.

"Yes," said Elinor Morgenthau. "An odd pair."

"An eccentric marriage, apparently."

"Eccentric marriage, eccentric people. Henry recommended him to Frank for the appointment to the Fed because Sargent was a brilliant economist. He did

warn Frank, though, that Sargent Peavy had a roving eye."

"Jessica says that Mrs. Peavy has not been a shy little wife."

Elinor laughed. "Oh, Eleanor! You won't believe the rumor Henry heard about her. He came home one day, absolutely roaring with laughter, and said— Well . . . He said that Letitia Peavy had a crush on J. Edgar Hoover! If it's true— Can you imagine a woman that naive? She *cannot* have *known!* Can you imagine a woman wanting to let that loathsome creature come near her?"

The First Lady could not but laugh, too. "Clyde Tolson would kill her," she said.

"Gossip holds that she has an inamorato: a highly prominent man. But they have been the soul of discretion, and no one is sure who he might be. All I've been able to learn is that he wears a uniform."

"And *Mister* Peavy? Prominent women?"

"Clare Boothe," said Elinor. "Maybe others. I don't know."

"Jessica says he broke off their affair a month ago. She says he had a new interest."

"Absolutely. A striking young redhead. I have no idea who she might be."

At ten, after Mrs. Roosevelt had changed into a navy-blue workaday dress and taken a cup of coffee and a

breakfast roll, and after she had answered half a dozen letters, she met with Lieutenant Edward Kennelly and Agent Stanlislaw Szczygiel. She had asked for a fresh pot of coffee from the kitchen and sat down with two men she knew would drink the coffee but would rather have something harder, even this early in the day.

"I realize that the presumption is strong that Jessica Dee murdered Sargent Peavy," said the First Lady. "But as you know, I have strong reservations. Do you mind if I use my chalkboard?"

Both men had seen her use her chalkboard before, and they smiled and nodded. The board stood on an easel, and she used white chalk to write on the black board.

"First," she said, "let's assume that Jessica did do it. I have problems with the evidence, but chiefly I have to wonder what was her motive. So . . ." She printed on the board—

(1) Jessica. But <u>why?</u> Cannot continue a love affair with a dead man. Heat of passion? But came with gun, gloves.

"What do I mean by that? Well, if she wanted to continue the love affair, what good would it do her to kill the man? If she killed him in the heat of passion because he had just announced he was terminating the

affair, how does it happen that she had brought with her a gun and the rubber gloves."

She began to print again—

(2) Mrs. Peavy, out of jealousy over Jessica or another woman.

(3) Jessica's new lover. To get rid of a rival for Jessica's affections.

(4) Mr. Peavy's new lover, for whatever reason.

(5) The husband or lover of that woman, out of jealousy.

(6) None of the above but someone who had reason to oppose some policy Mr. Peavy was advocating at the Federal Reserve Board.

"The Federal Reserve Board, gentlemen, has the power to make or break a business, or a whole line of businesses."

"The murderer has to be a woman," said Kennelly.

"Why?"

"Why else would he have been stark, staring naked?" Kennelly asked. "Would a man have come to kill him and forced him to strip before he shot him?"

"He might," said Mrs. Roosevelt, "if he wanted to create the impression that a woman committed the crime. A man might have broken into Jessica's apartment, stolen her earrings, and brought one with him to plant by the body."

"All right. Then why would the professor's seminal vesicles have been empty?"

"He was a sexually active man," said Mrs. Roosevelt. "In the hour before his death he might have visited a woman in a hotel room. He might, indeed, have visited a prostitute."

The President and the First Lady were presiding that evening over a formal state dinner, to welcome British Prime Minister Stanley Baldwin. The visit was slightly delicate, diplomatically, because the florid, outspoken Winston Churchill had arrived in New York a day earlier, to receive a popular welcome distinctly greater than Baldwin received. Crowds of people cheered Churchill. The newspapers generally welcomed him. Baldwin received a respectful but reserved greeting.

American diplomats had been instructed to explain this by reminding everyone that Churchill was the son of an American, Jenny Jerome of New York, and had risen to the very highest ranks in British politics in spite of being "half American." Stanley Baldwin was too shrewd a man to accept this explanation. He knew that a very large number of Americans embraced Churchill because of his shrill invective against Hitler, and he attributed this and to the influence of American Jews.

Baldwin suspected, too, that Churchill had ar-

ranged his visit to America to coincide with his own, to diminish his influence.

It was the President's habit to convene a cocktail party in the West Sitting Hall—the center hall of the private quarters—early every evening. Usually, these sessions were private and intimate, initiated by his calling out. *"Who's at home?"* Missy LeHand was there, invariably. So was Louis Howe, usually. Also present often were his personal physician and his military aide.

Mrs. Roosevelt did not usually sit down with the President at these cocktail hours. She did not, on the whole, approve of drinking, and she had observed the prohibition law as long as it was in effect—as the President most emphatically never had. Anyway, she found the conversation at the cocktail hour was usually frivolous.

Tonight, though, was different. The British Prime Minister was a guest in the White House and would join the President for cocktails. Because the cocktail hour would be followed by the formal dinner, the President and the male guests were dressed in white tie. The First Lady wore a rose-colored silk gown. Missy would not attend the formal dinner and was wearing workaday clothes. Louie Howe detested formal dinners and would dine elsewhere, alone. He sat down for the cocktail hour in an ash-smeared blue suit.

The British ambassador was present, as was Vice President John Nance Garner.

Two guests occasionally invited to the cocktail hour and invited to tonight's dinner filled out the informal occasion. They were presidential adviser Bernard Baruch and the Chairman of the new Securities and Exchange Commission, Joseph Kennedy. The President had his reasons for having this pair present. He felt it would be good for Stanley Baldwin to sit and chat with a Jew and an Irish Catholic.

There was maybe a second reason for inviting Kennedy. He had supplied the champagne for the dinner. White House dinners were notorious for the miserly quantity and the bad quality of the New York state champagne that was served. "One glass of swill and no refill," an editorialist had written. Joe Kennedy supplied fine champagne for an occasional dinner and the very finest of spirits for the President's private pantry—and had done so even when Prohibition remained in effect. Joe had never allowed the Volstead Act to stand in the way of making a tidy profit and influential friends.

Stanley Baldwin had the look and manner of the quintessential English country squire: solid and stolid, smoking a pipe. "Winston," he said to the President but loud enough that all could hear it, "is an altogether admirable fellow but opinionated and excitable. I shouldn't want to say we can't trust him; 'tisn't like

that at all; but one can never be sure what will inspire him next."

Mrs. Roosevelt would have liked to meet Winston Churchill. She had first heard his name when she was at school in England in 1899 and he was a correspondent in the Boer War. She remembered the thrill that went through the country when word came from South Africa that, having been captured by the Boers, he had escaped. He had seemed then to be a very romantic figure, and she suspected he would remain so now.

But it would be poor form to ask Stanley Baldwin about him.

When the cocktail hour was breaking up and the guests were turning toward the elevator hall to go down to dinner, Mrs. Roosevelt beckoned Joseph Kennedy to step apart with her for a moment's private conversation.

"I understand, Mr. Kennedy, that you were a close personal friend of Mr. Sargent Peavy."

The sandy-haired, somewhat ruddy-faced Kennedy regarded the First Lady from behind round, horn-rimmed eyeglasses, which gave him a distinctly owlish appearance. "I knew him in Boston. I can't say we were *close* friends, but I did think of him as a friend. When both of us came to Washington, we resumed that friendship."

"Did you know about his relationship with Jessica Dee?"

Kennedy smiled. "Oh, yes. Poor old Sarge. He fell heavily for her. You know her, I hear. You can see why. Eventually Letitia had to put her foot down about that."

"Do you think Jessica killed him?"

"Impossible!"

"She says he was already seeing another woman. What do you know about that, Mr. Kennedy?"

He laughed. "Sarge had an eye for beautiful women. His next one was Andrea Alphand."

"A redhead?"

"Absolutely. French, I understand. A journalist-type lady. I don't think she's been in this country very long."

"Thank you very much, Mr. Kennedy. Thank you very much indeed. Andrea Alphand . . ."

Before she went down to dinner, Mrs. Roosevelt went into her study and checked the name in the telephone directory. There was no listing for Andrea Alphand. She made two quick calls, one to Lieutenant Kennelly, who was still at his office, and one to Stanlislaw Szczygiel, for whom she left a message. She asked the two men to see what they could find out about a woman named Andrea Alphand.

V

THE PRESIDENT USUALLY TOOK his lunch at his desk, but on this Saturday he had it brought to the oval study adjacent to his bedroom, where he sat in a sweater and no necktie or jacket and worked on one of his stamp albums. Apart from his stamp collection, the oval study reflected another of his interests—it was decorated with paintings and models of sailing boats and ships. He had invited Mrs. Roosevelt to join him, and they shared a lunch of chicken salad, apples, and coffee.

The First Lady often chose these private moments to talk to the President about things that had engaged her interest, such as the geophagy she had learned about at her Wednesday breakfast. She would have liked to suggest a federal program to supplement the diets of people who ate clay, but she saw that the President was trying to relax after what she knew had been an exceptionally difficult week spent trying to goad a

recalcitrant Congress into action, so she decided to defer suggesting a program until later. She tried to keep the conversation in a light vein.

"I must tell you something that Senator La Follette said. He said that—"

"I noticed the two of you tête-à-tête," the President interrupted, chuckling.

"Well . . . We were talking about the income tax, and the senator said he thought the tax law should be written so that *every* American, no matter how poor, would pay a little income tax—because it would give every American a sense of having a share in government."

"An interesting philosophy, not unlike the Republican ideology."

She smiled. "I'm not sure I entirely follow that."

"Babs, I want to ask you something. Are you meddling in police business again?"

"Not meddling, no. I'm just trying to determine if Jessica Dee is indeed guilty of murdering Mr. Sargent Peavy. I find it difficult to believe that girl could have—"

"Why not let the police and the prosecutors and perhaps ultimately a court decide whether she did it or not?"

"Essentially that is what I am doing. I do have a few ideas, however, and, believe me, Lieutenant Kennelly is glad to hear them."

"Well . . . Just keep in mind, you can cause us a lot of embarrassment."

"I will certainly keep that in mind. May I ask you just one question about Mr. Peavy?"

"Just one," said the President, pulling off his pince-nez and beginning to wipe the lenses with a handkerchief.

"I am looking for a motive. Was Mr. Peavy the author of any significant new policy at the Federal Reserve Board? I mean, could anything he was doing there or advocating there have so affected some person or group as to create a motive for killing him?"

The President shook his head. "From what I hear, he was pretty much a go-along sort of fellow, a follower, not a leader. I suspect he was feeling his way."

The funeral for Sargent Peavy was held early Saturday afternoon at St. John's Church. It was attended by Mrs. Roosevelt as representative for the President, Henry and Elinor Morgenthau, Joseph and Rose Kennedy, Professor Felix Frankfurter representing the Harvard faculty, and many bankers and brokers and economists. Letitia was flanked by Peavy's father and brother.

Following the funeral the casket was driven to Union Station, where it was put aboard a train for Boston. Sargent Peavy would be buried Sunday afternoon.

Professor Letitia Peavy asked George Washington

University to advise her students that she would meet her classes on Tuesday.

In 1935 it was still possible for the President of the United States to relax on Saturday afternoon and part of Sunday. This Sunday morning, February 17, he met with Louis Howe to discuss ways of breaking the legislative logjam. That meeting was followed by one with Vice President John Nance Garner, Senator Hugo Black, and Congressmen Sam Rayburn, Emmanuel Celler, and John McCormack.

The meeting was discouraging. When it was over, the President wheeled himself to the elevator and returned to his private quarters, where he asked his valet to draw a bath for him and help him into the tub. He soaked for a while, then had himself helped out and helped to dress. He called Missy. She had just returned from church and would be glad to have lunch with him in his oval study. He called the kitchen and specifically demanded sandwiches made from thick slices of ham and thin slices of cheese, with lots of brown mustard. And beer.

Mrs. Nesbitt was away and so was the First Lady, so the kitchen staff followed his orders to the letter. The President and Missy sat down to what he called the first satisfying lunch he'd had from the White House kitchen in two weeks.

"You haven't forgotten your afternoon appointment, have you, Effdee?"

Missy called him Effdee, for the F and D in F.D.R. For years she had called him that—but only in the presence of people in his innermost circle: the ones he called "Babs" (the First Lady), "Louie" (Louis Howe), "the Hop" (Harry Hopkins), "Pa" (General Edwin Watson), and a few others. In other company she called him Mr. President. It amused him to notice how adroitly she switched back and forth between Effdee and Mr. President. The switches evidenced her infallible judgment of just how close to him people were. He had remarked once that he hadn't realized how good a friend a certain man was until he heard Missy call him Effdee in that man's presence.

"What appointment?"

"Mrs. Roosevelt has invited Dr. Joseph Rhine of Duke University to visit and present his theories."

"Theories on what?"

"Parapsychology. Psychokinesis."

"What in the name of—?"

"Parapsychology deals with attempts to learn whether or not some people have a power to communicate mentally, without speaking or giving any other signal. Psychokinesis deals with the ability of people to influence the movement of objects, without touching them."

The President nodded, then grinned. "Getting im-

movable objects to move," he laughed. "Maybe I could use that power on the Congress."

Dr. Rhine was a handsome man medium-size. His appealing personality suggested that he knew he had to deal constantly with skeptics and had to overcome their skepticism by being pleasantly persuasive.

He proposed that the President, Mrs. Roosevelt, and Missy take part in a simple little test. He had a special pack of twenty-five cards, imprinted in equal numbers with each of five symbols: a star, a square, a circle, a plus, and parallel wavy lines. For the experiment, one person would deal the cards and concentrate on the symbol. A second person would be so seated as to be unable to see the other person or the cards. The second person would try to guess what the first person was concentrating on and trying to communicate mentally.

Statistically, the second person should guess right five times out of twenty-five, twenty times out of a hundred and so on.

The President dealt the cards and concentrated on them. Mrs. Roosevelt concentrated on receiving his mental signal and knowing what he was looking at.

"Square . . . wavy lines . . . star . . . circle . . . wavy lines . . . square."

Mrs. Roosevelt guessed right six times out of twenty-five. They tried again, and she guessed five times. On the third try she guessed four times. On the

fourth try she guessed four times. For one hundred tries she guessed right nineteen times, which was statistically insignificant.

"I'm afraid you don't send a very clear signal, Franklin."

"To the contrary," he said, laughing, "I send a very clear signal. You just don't receive it."

Then he tried communicating with Missy. She guessed right thirty-one times out of a hundred.

"You see, Babs?" said the President. "The problem is not with me as a transmitter, it is with you as a receiver.

Dr. Rhine explained that for the test to be experimentally valid they would have to go through thousands of guesses.

"We have found some individuals who constantly exceed mathematical probability," he said. "Also, we have found individuals who consistently roll dice with results that defy the odds. We believe that is evidence of psychokinesis."

"Do you regard the experimental results as conclusive?" asked Mrs. Roosevelt.

"Not conclusive," said Dr. Rhine. "We continue the experiments."

"Very interesting, Brother Rhine," said the President. "Have you given any thought to what use mankind might make of this?"

"I'll think about that when I manage to prove the powers really do exist," said Rhine.

On Monday morning, Mrs. Roosevelt met again with Kennelly and Szczygiel. She had coffee for them, as always, and they sat facing her chalkboard, where she had crossed off item number six.

"The President tells me Mr. Peavy was doing nothing much as a member of the Board of Governors of the Federal Reserve," she said. "It would seem extremely unlikely he gave anyone cause to want to murder him."

"I wouldn't eliminate the possibility entirely," said Kennelly.

"I don't," said Mrs. Roosevelt. "That's why I just drew a line through the words and did not erase them. So . . . Has either of you learned anything about Miss Andrea Alphand?"

"No," said Kennelly. "We have no record of her. She has no telephone, no account with the electric company, no driver's license in the District or in Virginia or Maryland."

"I've made some calls," said Szczygiel. "I spoke to the security officer at the French embassy. He wired Paris. The French government has no record of ever having issued a passport in the name Andrea Alphand. The French are very meticulous about these things. They keep card files that fill warehouses, and they are

going to check to see what record they have, if any, of a French citizen by that name."

"Excellent, Mr. Szczygiel!" said Mrs. Roosevelt.

"Well . . . I'm not sure where it gets us. I also called the several French newspapers and press agencies. None of them has ever heard of Andrea Alphand."

"The mystery deepens," said the First Lady. "Allow me to change the subject. I am sure you are aware of how things come to prey on your mind, how ideas suddenly occur to you and interrupt your sleep. Well . . . I have had such an experience. Something Mrs. Peavy said to me. I asked her a question almost casually. She answered almost casually. But her answer troubles me. It came to me yesterday morning. I didn't telephone you gentlemen yesterday. It isn't that urgent. But—"

"What did she say, Ma'am?" asked Szczygiel.

"I asked her where she was when Mr. Peavy was murdered. She said she was in her car, driving from the university to her home. How long could that drive take? Fifteen minutes? How could she know he was killed in that quarter of an hour?"

"She couldn't," said Kennelly.

"Exactly. So why did she say he was?"

Kennelly grinned. "You suggest the evidence against Jessica Dee is flimsy. Well, I wouldn't want to go to trial against Mrs. Peavy on the evidence of that statement."

"Touché, Lieutenant," said Mrs. Roosevelt.

• • •

Once again varying her habit, the First Lady stopped in on the President's early-evening cocktail party. It was spare that night. Besides the President and Mrs. Roosevelt, only Louis Howe, Harry Hopkins, and Missy LeHand were present.

As a variation on his usual martinis, the President mixed a rum cocktail. It was a concoction he had learned about in Haiti when he had gone there as President Wilson's assistant secretary of the navy. In a shaker he mixed one part rum, one part fresh-squeezed orange juice, some brown sugar, and some egg white, all poured over crushed ice and vigorously shaken. The other ingredients disguised the rum, and innocent guests often drank more of these cocktails than they should have.

It amused the President that he was able occasionally to get his mother tipsy. He had done the same to the First Lady, until she caught on and became cautious about the drink. The other guests—Missy, the Hop, and Louie—didn't care about getting a bit smashed and drank the tasty mixture happily.

The President loved a good story. He had traveled to Trenton, New Jersey, to commemorate some element of the Battle of Trenton. A noisy motorcade led by smoky motorcycles had carried him in an open car from the railroad station through the streets of Tren-

ton. A Jersey politician had come to him afterward
with this story—

A little boy of four years or so had been sitting on
his father's shoulders in the crowd. As the President
passed by, the father had tried to get the child to focus
his attention on the great man. But the little boy was
far more interested in something else and would only
glance at the President. "Oh, look, Eddy!" the father
had said. "That's President Roosevelt! You'll always
remember the day you saw the President of the United
States." But the little boy's attention was firmly fixed
on something else. His father kept urging him to look
at the President, and finally the little boy said, with
some impatience, "Don' care 'bout no pwesident. Want
to look at the moootooocycoos!"

Having sipped sparingly from a rum cocktail, Mrs.
Roosevelt left the party and went on to her evening
appointment: a dinner being held by the International
Ladies' Garment Workers Union.

An editorialist commented the next morning—

True to form, La Eleanor dined luxuriously last
evening in the company of her socialist pals Dave
Dubinsky and Sid Hillman. All three of them, it
must not be forgotten, are listed in Mrs. Dilling's
The Red Network, a handbook for patriots, identifying the nation's most dangerous Communist
conspirators. When these three meet, lovers of

liberty must become alert. What schemes they were hatching last night over so proletarian a dinner as breast of pheasant with wild rice would defy imagination. Working people sitting down over fatback and beans might well wonder.

Tommy Thompson had marked the editorial, and Mrs. Roosevelt read it in the morning.

"That asinine book keeps coming up," said Tommy, referring to *The Red Network*, which had been out nearly a year.

"Actually," said Mrs. Roosevelt, "I am pleased and honored to be mentioned in Mrs. Dilling's book and should have been disappointed if I had not been mentioned. After all, how often does one have the honor of being listed among such distinguished men as Senator William Borah, Ambassador William Bullitt, Chiang Kai-shek, Professor Felix Frankfurter, H. L. Mencken, and Mahatma Gandhi?"

In mid-morning, Tuesday, the First Lady met with Stanlislaw Szczygiel. The Secret Service agent sat down, crossed his legs, and opened a leather file.

"I've spent some time," he said, "looking into the . . . How shall we call it? The *non-amatory* aspects of the life of Mr. Sargent Peavy. He had an interesting and apparently honorable career."

"I should expect so," said Mrs. Roosevelt. "I am

sure the President checked into that thoroughly before he appointed him."

"He was born in Hartford, Connecticut, the son of a Congregational minister. In fact, he was descended from a long line of Congregational parsons. His brother is one, too. He prepped at Groton, then went on to Yale, where he was initiated into Skull and Bones in 1911. He earned his doctorate at Yale, then was invited to join the Harvard faculty."

"What about military service? Wasn't he of draft age during the World War?"

Szczygiel shook his head. "No record of it. I assume he had some minor physical deficiency."

"He seems to have been well respected at Harvard."

"I am sure he was. His record there is simply one of steady advancement. He is the author of three well-read books on economics, one of them a textbook for undergraduates. Besides that he published a dozen or so monographs in various learned journals. His reputation at Harvard was that of a quiet, industrious scholar, a respected teacher, and an all-'round good fellow. It was rumored of him that he had some amorous adventures, but if he did he was most discreet about them and did not damage his career."

"Did you find anything, Mr. Szczygiel, that might suggest a motive for murdering him?"

"A remote possibility. A *very* remote possibility. I

spoke at length by telephone last evening with a federal bank examiner in Boston. Mr. Peavy was associated with some men who are in trouble. But *he* was not. There will be indictments. But he would not have been indicted."

"Can you be specific?"

"As a respected economist, Sargent Peavy was asked to be a member of the board of directors of several banks. One of those banks was the Cabot National Bank of Boston. The bank failed shortly before the President was inaugurated and declared the bank holiday in 1933. It failed because of alleged criminal misconduct by its officers."

"Did it take two years to find that out?" asked Mrs. Roosevelt.

"Yes. There have been so many bank failures since 1929 that the examiners have fallen far behind in their work. Cabot was not a big bank. It did not have priority. But now—"

"Just what did its officers do that broke the law and caused it to fail?"

"They made bad loans," said Szczygiel. "Insufficiently secured loans. To cronies. Probably taking payoffs. I need hardly remind you that there are some prominent bankers in Sing Sing and other prisons, for doing just that."

"How is it that Mr. Peavy would not have been indicted, if the others are likely to be?"

"The examiners have reviewed the minutes of the meetings of the board of directors. There are probably five dozen or so suspicious loans. Peavy voted no on every one of them."

"Why?"

"The minutes don't say; they just record the ayes and nays."

"How does this relate to the murder?"

"Peavy would not have been indicted. But he would have been called as a witness and required to testify as to why he voted as he did. He could have testified about the discussions in the directors' meetings. He might have been the witness who would have sunk the officers and directors of the Cabot National Bank of Boston."

VI

I AM SORRY TO trouble you, Mr. Kennedy," said Mrs. Roosevelt, "but it occurred to me that you probably know more about Boston banking than any other man in Washington. After all, you made your fortune as a banker."

Kennedy grinned. "Or as a bootlegger. The other story is that I made my money as a bootlegger."

"My husband would not have appointed you to your present position if he had believed that."

Kennedy had a wide, infectious grin, which he showed rarely. "Actually," he said with a subdued chuckle, "he appointed me because of the $25,000 I contributed to his campaign."

Mrs. Roosevelt smiled tolerantly. "That, Mr. Kennedy, would not have won you appointment to the chairmanship of the Securities and Exchange Commission if the President had thought you had earned your fortune illegally."

Because of the clutter of work Tommy Thompson was doing for the First Lady in her study, Mrs. Roosevelt was meeting with Joseph Kennedy in the Red Room, one of the state rooms on the first floor of the White House. As she always did when she received a visitor, she had ordered coffee from the kitchen, which had been brought with a small assortment of vanilla wafers and crisp little cookies.

"I should like to talk with you about Mr. Sargent Peavy," said Mrs. Roosevelt. "I believe you and he were friends, were you not?"

Kennedy nodded. "Yes. We were contemporaries. He was just three years younger than I. He and Letitia were guests in our home from time to time, and Rose and I were guests in theirs. They were *fun* people. They enjoyed a good time. They enjoyed drinking and smoking and dancing. They were always welcome at parties. They were always ready to take part in games. I remember a masquerade ball. The Peavys showed up dressed as *saltimbanques* or Harlequins—you know: multicolored tights and grotesque masks. They had bought these costumes in Paris, from real *saltimbanques*, brought them home, and waited for an occasion to wear them. Ladies who had come as Marie Antoinette or Martha Washington thought Letitia's knit tights were scandalous.

"I don't mean to indulge in gossip, but I understand it wasn't an ideal marriage," Mrs. Roosevelt suggested.

"I have to say that depends entirely on how you define ideal marriage," said Kennedy. "They strayed. He especially. But they remained married for seventeen years. They had their adventures, but their affairs were only adventures. They remained devoted to each other."

"Until Miss Dee came along."

"Well . . . Yes, Sarge did develop a special fascination for Jessica. You can see why."

"My questions about Mr. Peavy really relate more to his activities as a banker," said Mrs. Roosevelt. "I understand he was a director of the Cabot National Bank of Boston and that there is a distinct possibility that other directors and officers of that bank will be indicted for fraud."

Kennedy nodded. "Very likely. The bank made improper loans to friends of the officers and directors."

"But it seems Mr. Peavy would not have been indicted."

"Sarge was a director of several banks. His name gave prestige to a board: distinguished economist and all that. Of course he resigned all those directorships when the President appointed him to the Fed."

"Did any of his other banks make improper loans?"

"Not enough to break them. But Sarge knew how to protect himself. If he regarded a loan as questionable, he voted no. The minutes of the board meetings would show he voted no."

"Was Cabot an unusual bank?" she asked.

"Well— I'd have to say yes. It embarrasses me to say it, but some of the Boston Irish involved in the bank were . . . men of less than sterling integrity. I've been called a bootlegger. The truth is, I got my franchises to sell some of the most distinguished brands of Scotch and so on *after* Repeal." He grinned and shrugged. "Of course, I kept my own cellar well stocked during the bluenose years—mine and those of some of my friends. But I didn't sell. Not then. I can't say the same for some of the officers of the bank."

"Are you saying that loans from Cabot National Bank of Boston went to buy illegal liquor?"

Kennedy smiled tolerantly. "To the contrary. Bootleggers *deposited* in the bank. But seeing Repeal coming, they wanted to buy into other lines of business. It was then that they turned to the bank for loans. The problem was that they had insufficient collateral. And the bank made the loans anyway."

"Because they were all friends," Mrs. Roosevelt suggested.

"Precisely. One hand washes the other, as they say."

"Mr. Peavy did not notify the banking authorities that—"

"Sarge would have done that if they had let him see that a loan was absolutely illegal. No, I think we

can count on it that he was an honest director, if maybe a little naive."

The First Lady shook her head skeptically.

"Let me give you an example," said Kennedy. "A major bootlegger in Boston was a man named Viscardi. He and his men brewed beer. When you are a brewer, what do you need, above all?"

"A brewery," said Mrs. Roosevelt.

"Good. But what I was thinking about was *trucks.* You have to deliver your beer, which means trucks. Seeing Repeal coming, Viscardi decided to go into the trucking business. He owned a dozen or so trucks, but that was not enough to become a major trucker—and major was all a man with his pride was going to be—so he needed to buy another twenty-five or thirty trucks. He tried to float a loan. The trouble was, Repeal was going to make the brewery worthless. He didn't have enough collateral. But he had friends at Cabot. He pledged the trucks he had, worth no more than, say, $8,000, borrowed $20,000, spent $18,000 for new trucks, and kicked back $2,000 to certain officers of the bank. Sarge Peavy voted no in the directors' meeting. He was suspicious of the deal, doubted it was a good investment, but I'm sure he didn't understand it was a complete fraud."

It is too bad he wasn't more perspicacious.

"There will be prosecutions," said Kennedy. "Sarge would have been a witness."

"Motive enough to kill him . . ." the First Lady mused.

"Motive enough to kill him," Kennedy agreed.

"This is very interesting," said Mrs. Roosevelt. "It adds a whole new dimension to the case."

"Maybe it will relieve some of the pressure on poor little Jessica," said Kennedy.

That evening when the President wheeled himself into the second-floor sitting room and called out "Who's home?" Missy and Louie appeared and were joined shortly by naval captain Ross McIntire, who had been assigned to the White House as the President's personal physician. McIntire was a plump easygoing fellow, and the President enjoyed his company even if he was the man who gave him painful shots in the hip every day.

Mrs. Roosevelt greeted them, then hurried on. She was on her way to a dinner to raise funds to provide medical assistance to the malnourished children of southern sharecroppers. It was being held at the Mayflower Hotel. Though she had to take along a Secret Service agent, she drove her own car.

A cocktail reception was in progress when she arrived. She was offered and accepted a small glass of sherry. Her host for the evening was Senator Carter Glass, who guided her around the room and introduced her to some of the famous people present. Most

of them were members of Congress and judges, but some were from show business and journalism.

The first man to whom Glass introduced her was H. L. Mencken, called "the sage of Baltimore," a salty, opinionated reporter, editorialist, and—probably most famously—author of *The American Language*. Mencken had a schooner of beer in his left hand and somehow managed to smoke a pipe while keeping his right free for shaking.

"It is a pleasure to see you again, Mr. Mencken." She had met him at the Democratic Convention in 1932, which he had covered for the *Baltimore Sun*. "As I recall, you had a large beer in your hand when I first met you though Prohibition was still in force at the time."

"Prohibition," Mencken growled through a grin. "I paid about as much attention to that as did Mr. Roosevelt."

Mrs. Roosevelt smiled. "It was the law," she said.

"When *Boobus Americanus*, hookworm-belt manifestation particularly, votes his heart, the Good Lord alone knows what will wind up in Congress or a state legislature, to produce what inanities of legislation."

Carter Glass smiled weakly and nodded.

"Think of it," said Mencken. "Huey Long's a senator! And he calls Senator Glass dirty names."

It was true. The Kingfish had loosed a vicious ver-

bal assault on the veteran senator. Now Glass nodded with animation. "He's a guttersnipe."

"Louisiana shouldn't be represented in Congress," pronounced Mencken. "The states of the Confederacy should not have been readmitted to the Union until they demonstrated that they could civilize themselves—a treatment Virginia never needed, incidentally, Senator, since it has always been civilized."

"Most adroit, Mr. Mencken," said the First Lady with a broad smile. Mencken had amended an insult to the senator from Virginia before Glass had time to take offense. "Most agile."

Mencken laughed. "I have to be conversationally agile, my dear lady. Otherwise—"

"Otherwise someone would shoot him," said Glass, who always spoke from the left corner of his mouth and was known for his ability to drip sarcasm. "Henry, I've got to present Mrs. Roosevelt to some others. Excuse us, please."

Mrs. Roosevelt had already noticed the man toward whom the senator now led her. He was W. C. Fields.

Senator Glass introduced her, and she said, "It is a pleasure to meet you, Mr. Dukenfield." She rarely addressed anyone by a nickname or pseudonym, and she knew that Fields's real name was William Claude Dukenfield. "I once saw you juggle."

"Juggle . . . Yaas. Yaas. That's how I got started in show biz. Juggler. Yaas."

"You were, as I recall, billed as 'The Eccentric Juggler,' and you wore a tramp costume."

" 'Eccentric.' Yaas. Yaas, I was. Very eccentric. Went all over the world with that act. South Africa . . . Australia."

"I saw you in London," said Mrs. Roosevelt. "You had an assistant, a girl who wore rather formal clothing—necktie, white shirt, vest, tailcoat—but then exposed her legs in black tights with a single ribbon garter."

"That was Hattie," said Fields. "She's my wife."

"Well, give her my best."

"Can't do that, I'm afraid. Haven't seen Hattie for years. She's content to receive checks from me."

"Anyway, it is a real pleasure to meet you. I've never forgotten your marvelous juggling."

"Juggling, yaas. Well . . . Incidentally, Mrs. R, the name really isn't Dukenfield. I had it legally changed in nineteen-ought-eight."

"Then you really are Mr. Fields."

"Not exactly. I had it changed from Dukenfield to Field. William C. Field. W. C. Field. But the theater managers persisted in putting W. C. Fields on the marquee, and finally I gave up and called myself Fields. Life plays funny tricks."

"It does indeed, Mr. Field."

Senator Glass then introduced her to Jean Harlow, whom she addressed as Miss Carpentier. Jean Harlow was Harlean Carpentier. She was genuinely glad to meet the First Lady, but her conversation was bland.

"I'm supposed to say funny things, or tough things, but that's all written for me. I don't come up with that kind of stuff myself."

Lieutenant Ed Kennelly had just stubbed out his last office Lucky and locked his desk drawer when the call came that there had been a shooting homicide in Washington Southeast. Wearily he telephoned his wife to say he would be late, probably very late. He was one of only two real homicide specialists in the department, and if they had not reached him at the office they would have called him at home. He lit a fresh cigarette.

He shrugged himself into the harness that held his shoulder holster. He pulled the clip from his .38 Colt automatic, and pulled back the slide to eject the cartridge from the chamber. Then he aimed at his desk and pulled the trigger. The hammer snapped. He pulled the slide twice more and snapped the automatic two more times. Finally he reloaded the pistol and set the safety. Automatics had a way of jamming if they were not cycled often, and he took no chances with his.

He switched on the two blinking red lights that sat

between the headlights on his Ford and set out for the crime scene. The Ford was a Model A, what Ford called a "cabriolet," and was a coupe with a rumble seat. He sounded his siren a few times and ran a few traffic signals and arrived at K Street about 9:20 P.M.

Kennelly knew the neighborhood well. It was a block of noisy, smoky bars. The bars on the south side of the street filled early in the evening, with Negroes chiefly. All but one of the bars on the north side had signs in the window, saying "We cater to the white race only." Sometimes the customers from the two kinds of bars met on the street for raucous yelling matches, and occasionally a free-swinging fistfight ensued. Rarely was anyone hurt, because the swinging fighters were almost invariably so drunk they could not land an effective punch.

Prostitutes black and white flounced along the sidewalks and did brisk business. They sewed little lead weights into the hems of their loose skirts, and when they pirouetted the skirts flew and exposed their underwear—and sometimes more because they weren't wearing any.

Moralists maintained a shrill and constant demand that the block be more severely policed and the block of vice be cleaned up.

But it was the alleys behind the bars that most concerned the Washington police. There, bar customers who stepped out the back door to relieve themselves

were often sapped and relieved of their money. There, in dark shadows, illicit substances were sold. There, in the light of dawn, a prone figure now and then turned out not to be just a very sick drunk sleeping off a hangover on the muddy ground but in fact a dead man.

Kennelly drove slowly into the alley behind the north side of K Street, showing his red lights. Two patrol cars waited for him, shining their headlights on a man lying face down at the edge of a puddle. His body was on the gravel pavement of the alley, and his head was half submerged in filthy water. A pearl-gray fedora lay in the water.

"Loo," said one of the uniformed officers. It was their slang for lieutenant. "Except to check to make sure he's dead, we haven't touched him."

"Well, let's touch him now," said Kennelly. "Turn him over."

"Uh . . . First, look what's there."

Some four feet from the outstretched hand of the body lay a snub-nosed revolver.

Kennelly nodded. "Let's turn him over."

They turned the body face up. He was a relatively young man, probably in his thirties. He had a thin moustache and a sharp chin and nose. He wore a camel overcoat with white buttons and a natty double-breasted suit, dark blue with pinstripes. His thin-soled, pointy-toed black shoes were protected by buttoned

gray spats. His silk shirt had been white, but it was slickly red now. Blood still oozed out. He had been taken down by shots dead-center to the chest.

Kennelly pulled on rubber gloves and explored the pockets of the suit.

"Well, if that ain't a hell of a note. Looka this. Cash. Lots of it. And not a shred of identification."

There were hundred-dollar bills soaked with blood, eighteen of them, plus another hundred fifty or so in smaller bills.

Kennelly went inside four bars that backed up on that alley. Of course, no one had heard any shots. No one had noticed a man in a dapper camel overcoat and pearl-gray fedora.

The revolver proved to be a .38 caliber Smith & Wesson. Two of the cartridges in its cylinder had been fired.

"It looks like he got off a couple of shots at whoever killed him," said Kennelly. "I wonder if he hit the guy."

On Wednesday morning the First Lady sat down with Tommy Thompson and again experimented with writing a column. She wrote—

Someone has been so kind as to send me the gift of a large globe-shaped fish bowl with two gold-fish with spectacular lacy tails and fins. As I

watch those two fish swimming 'round and 'round, it occurs to me that they have absolutely no privacy.

Living in the White House is something like that.

Tommy stopped taking dictation and answered the telephone. Lieutenant Kennelly was calling.

"We need to talk to Jessica Dee again," he said. "I thought maybe you would like to call her. She might be more receptive to questions from you."

"What questions need we ask her, Lieutenant?"

"Something very odd has happened. A man was shot to death in an alley behind K Street last night. We sent the slugs from the body to the ballistics lab. Those slugs were fired from the same gun that killed Sargent Peavy."

"I should think that exonerates Jessica," said Mrs. Roosevelt.

"It does if she can account for her whereabouts at the time of the shooting."

"What time?"

"About eight-thirty," said Kennelly.

"Well, I would be happy to call Jessica and ask her where she was. Who was killed?"

"A Boston gunsel by the name of Vito Francione, also known as Frankie One."

"What possible connection could there be between—?"

"For right now, nothing but the gun. But the ballistics tests are certain; Frankie One was killed with the same gun that killed Sargent Peavy."

"Which could not have been Jessica," Mrs. Roosevelt said firmly.

"Well. There's another question I'd like to have answered. Does Jessica have any kind of wound?"

"Wound?"

"Frankie got off two shots before he was dropped. Couple of my fellows looking over the area in the light of day found bloodstains on the gravel of the alley. Looks like the shooter might have stumbled to the end of the alley and got into a car. If Jessica has a gunshot wound . . . Well, you figure."

"I will telephone her right now, Lieutenant."

First she called Harry Hopkins. He would be working on Capitol Hill that morning, trying to round up votes for the Social Security Bill; and she asked him to stop by Senator Long's office and see if he could detect any sign of a wound on Jessica Dee.

Then she called Jessica.

"Mrs. Roosevelt," Jessica said on the phone, "I have never fired a gun in my life. Not even once."

"You can simplify everything, Jessica—even exonerating yourself completely in the death of Sargent

Peavy—if you will tell me where you were last evening."

"Oh, Mrs. Roosevelt! I was at the same place I was *last* Tuesday evening. And you know I can't tell you where that was."

VII

THE WEDNESDAY EDITION OF the *Washington Post* contained a story that distressed Mrs. Roosevelt. It was not on the front page, and she did not notice it until Tommy pointed it out to her.

FBI TAKES OVER INVESTIGATION OF PEAVY MURDER

J. Edgar Hoover, Chief of the Federal Bureau of Investigation, announced this morning that he will assume responsibility, beginning immediately, for the investigation of the unsolved murder of Sargent Peavy, late member of the Board of Governors of the Federal Reserve Bank.

"The murder is a week old," he noted, "and it is time for the professional investigators of the FBI to take over and close the case."

An angry First Lady made it plain to Missy that she wanted to talk to the President and wanted to talk to him *now*. Missy had seen Mrs. Roosevelt angry only once or twice before, and she slipped her directly into the Oval Office, ahead of the President's next appointment.

"It is intolerable, Franklin, that that abhorrent degenerate should question the competence of the honest officers of the D.C. police and the Secret Service. He is nothing but a nauseating, grandstanding publicity hound."

The President grinned. "I hear he's like a beat cop who lifts apples from fruit stands. He walks out of restaurants without paying his bills." The President shrugged. "So, I am told, does that immaculate all-American hero Elliott Ness."

"Louie has explained to you our interest in Jessica Dee," said Mrs. Roosevelt. "If Hoover got his sticky fingers on that—It mustn't be allowed to happen."

"You and Louie did nothing wrong?"

"Of course not. But what might that baneful man try to make of it?"

Ten minutes later a messenger left the White House carrying a message to J. Edgar Hoover. It was a clipping of the story, with a curt note at the end—

"The murder is a week old," he noted, "and it is time for the professional investigators of the FBI to take over."

Brother John—

No.

FDR

When Mrs. Roosevelt returned to her office, Tommy said she'd had a call from Harry Hopkins. Jessica Dee looked in perfect condition to him, he said. He could see no sign or a wound or injury. Mrs. Roosevelt called Lieutenant Kennelly to tell him that and to tell him the FBI would not be sticking its nib in.

"We know a little more about Frankie One," said Kennelly. "He has a police record. The worst item on it is a three-year term in Massachusetts for assault with a deadly weapon. Apart from that he's done some jail time for beating up on people. My guess is, he was a collector—that is, he collected money owed to loan sharks and bookies."

"He was then what I believe is sometimes called a legbreaker," she suggested.

"You know a lot more than a lady—especially a First Lady—might be expected to know about such things."

. . .

That afternoon snow began to fall. By three o'clock
the lawns around the White House were covered by
four or five inches of it, and that profound silence that
accompanies a gentle snowfall descended on Washington. Following long-standing Washington custom,
offices closed an hour early to let people make their
way home before the snowfall accumulated so much
as to disrupt traffic.

Washington was not a city equipped to deal with
much snow. It was in fact a Southern city and moved
at a Southern pace, with generally Southern social at-
titudes. Its black population was called "colored" or
Negro—and not infrequently by an unkind word. Only
that word was considered impolite. Even the word
coon was thought of as an amiable joke.

Washington was a strictly segregated city in 1935.
Even so, thousands of blacks continued to come,
many having heard that the Depression was over in
the capital city. There were, in fact, jobs to be had in
Washington, as New Deal agencies proliferated and
hired. But almost none of those jobs were for blacks.
A few were hired as janitors and porters, none as
clerks or secretaries or administrators.

The colored still rode strictly in the rear seats of
trolley cars and buses. The fare was a nickel, and a
government employee sent on an errand to another
part of the city drew two nickels from petty cash—

leaving a receipt—for fare going and coming. Major Dwight Eisenhower, going up to Capitol Hill from the War Department to deliver documents to members of Congress did just this: signed a chit for two nickels.

That snowy Wednesday evening, Mrs. Roosevelt was guest of honor at a dinner meeting of the NAACP, at which Mary McLeod Bethune would also be a guest. At about five she telephoned to learn if the meeting had been postponed because of the snow and found out that it had not. She left early, so as not to be late, and allowed herself to be driven in a government car.

Since no hotel that would serve colored had a dining room big enough to accommodate the number of guests expected, the dinner was held in the gymnasium of a colored high school, where the tables were set up on the basketball floor. The food was carried in cars from the kitchen of a nearby church.

Mrs. Roosevelt felt she had never seen such exuberance and optimism. But she was embarrassed by the reception she received: respectful and warm and generous.

Looking out the windows of the Oval Office, the President had seen the snow falling. It made him think of boyhood days on the Hudson, when snow had covered the ice on the river. He remembered with particular fondness his ice boat, with great sail and slick runners, on which he had sped across the ice, across and up

and down the broad stream. His mother had watched with horror what she regarded as a dangerous sport, his father with enthusiasm and admiration for his athletic son.

He repaired to the second floor and called in his intimates for the cocktail hour. Tonight it was Missy and Louie and Harry the Hop, no one else. The President shook martinis. He had become a little more daring about their mixture and now mixed them five to one. In any case, it was a ritual he immensely enjoyed, and he was as careful about the measuring and blending of the gin and vermouth as a pharmacist mixing a prescription medicine.

"I've got to read you a letter," the President said when the drinks were poured. He took from his pocket a small sheet of light-blue writing paper on which a letter had been composed with a pencil. "It is from Brother—catch that, 'Brother'—Billy Bob Fox, pastor of the Church of the Redeemer, Lubbock, Texas. Here's what Brother Billy Bob has to say—

'Dear Mister Sir,
'I read by the news that boys in CCC camps are eloud to play at cards in their berucks after work. Sherly this cannot be true! Playing at cards is Saytans work! Them boys sools will bern in hellfire. Please write back and tell me all the cards will be got rid of and the boys will spend there time insted

reading of the Hooly Skriptcher. I pray for you every day and every night, just the way I pray for our kuntry.

                    'Revrund Brother Billy Bob Fox.'

"Missy . . . Answer that for me, will you?"

Missy nodded. She had already composed an answer in her mind. She would tell the Reverend Billy Bob that the President was not aware that cards were played in CCC camps and would make every effort to see to it that Bibles were distributed to every barracks. After which she would file the reverend's letter in the round file.

The President had his valet help him into his bath, soaked for a while in hot water, then was assisted to his bed, where he lay on his stomach for a massage. When he was dressed in his pajamas and propped up against pillows, he rang Missy's suite on the third floor, and she came down for dinner.

Again tonight, Missy wore her dark-blue silk nightgown and her sheet white peignoir. The President called the kitchen for their dinners, having no confidence anything palatable would be delivered. Missy placed an album of records on the table beside the phonograph. She turned the crank to wind up the machine, then put the first record on the turntable and lowered the arm. The President loved Antonín Dvořák's *Symphony from the New World,* and that was the piece she had chosen to play during their dinner.

．　．　．

Ed Kennelly was well known in the bars along K Street
as an honest cop but a tough man who took no non-
sense. When he asked a question he expected an answer. He had been called a nosebreaker. What was
more to the point, he was a man who could close a
bar where the bartender did not give him quick,
straight answers. He had more than once strode behind a bar, snatched down the license, torn it to bits,
then announced the bar was closed because it didn't
have a license. On other occasions he had shoved the
license in his pocket, closed the bar because it could
not show a license, and carried the license to his office, where it would wait for a visit by the owner—
with the information Kennelly wanted.

He trudged in out of the snow and walked up to
the bar in a spot called O'Reilly's. It was an old-
fashioned saloon, with some of the character of an
Irish pub. The bartender was the owner, O'Reilly, a
burly man with a big belly. He drew a beer and pushed
it across the bar to the big Irish detective.

"Do for ya, Kennelly?" he asked.

Kennelly nodded. He handed O'Reilly a copy of
Frankie One's morgue photo. "Know this guy?"

"He's been in here. Sure. He's been in. He's the stiff
they found in the alley, I guess."

"Right. Naturally, I've got a curiosity about how
that party got dead."

"Me, too. It ain't good for business for guys to get dropped in the alley out back."

"Whatta ya know about him, O'Reilly?"

O'Reilly shook his head. "I never saw him before . . . let's say a week ago. I saw him . . . let's say twice . . . maybe three times. I'd just as soon from the start I never saw him at all. Bad-news kind of guy, y' know?"

Kennelly picked up his beer and took a long, appreciative draft. "Like how?"

O'Reilly reached under the bar and pulled out a small beer of his own. It had always amused Kennelly how O'Reilly liked his beer warm. "Swaggers. The guy swaggers. He's wearin' this camel overcoat that had to cost four times what any other guy's overcoat cost. And the way he looked around, at other guys, I'd have sworn he was packin' heat. I mean, like he just sort of defied anybody to look crossways at him."

"A mean son of a bitch . . ."

"That's how I read him."

"He meet anybody? Talk to anybody?"

O'Reilly shook his head. "I got the impression he was lookin' for somebody, but whoever it was, he didn't find him in here."

Kennelly took from his pocket a mug shot of Jessica Dee and showed it to O'Reilly.

The bar owner shook his head emphatically. "I know who *she* is. I saw her picture in the paper. I

swear to ya, Kennelly, she was never in my place. And I'd know if she was. A babe like that's *conspicuous* in a joint like this. She's got class. She'd get a twenty-dollar offer in five minutes."

"Well, thanks for the beer, O'Reilly."

"Any time, Kennelly. Any time."

In the town of Washington, snow tended to turn to slush very quickly. Dirty slush. It was pleasant for a few hours, then pleasant no more. When Kennelly left O'Reilly's and moved along the street to a bar called The Blue Diamond, the tires of passing cars were throwing slush against the ones parked on the street.

He'd gone to O'Reilly's first because he had a little more confidence in O'Reilly than he had in the keepers of the other joints on this block. He had no confidence in the operators of The Blue Diamond.

The place was garish, under dim blue and pink lights that hardly pierced the heavy haze of cigarette smoke that all but choked even a habitual smoker like Kennelly. In O'Reilly's the crowd was jovial; here it was silent and sullen, drinking assiduously at the bar and in flimsy wooden booths. A tipsy girl danced on the bar, her skirt hiked to her waist, and drew no applause and almost no attention.

"Got an entertainment license, Rudy?" Kennelly asked the bartender dryly.

The bartender, Rudy, shoved a beer across the bar and shook his head. "She doesn't work here. Strictly amateur."

"Got insurance, in case she falls off the bar?"

"Her friends'll catch her."

"Not if she falls off the back."

Rudy shrugged. "She's done it a dozen times and never fell. Poor kid's starved for attention, and even with that she doesn't get it."

Kennelly showed the morgue photo of Frankie One. "Know this guy?"

Rudy, who had the unmistakable appearance of a man who had spent time in prison—pallid, emaciated, furtive, tattooed—shook his head. "I don't know the guy. I seen him. I seen him in here. Jesus! That's a morgue picture! He the guy they found in the alley?"

"That's him."

Rudy frowned over the photograph. "Yeah . . . yeah. I seen him in here two or three times the last week or so. Shivery guy. Ya know what I mean? Scary."

"Like how?"

"Lieutenant, you know me. I spent some time around scary guys. This fella was a guy I'd keep away from, wherever I saw him. Guy like him gives me the willies."

Kennelly handed Rudy the mug shot of Jessica Dee.

Rudy glanced at the drunken girl staggering on the bar. The other bartender snapped his fingers at her and gestured that she should climb down. Rudy shook his

head. "For just a minute, I thought . . . But no. For sure. I never seen this chick. Not to say she couldn't have been in here and I didn't see her. Anyway, the scary guy had another broad. I seen him with her twice, I suppose. Hey! You want to see a broad, find her. Lemme tell ya. Ya can't miss her. Ain't no other broad looks like that broad. She's one of a kind."

"Like how?"

"Hey!" Rudy used his hands to outline an hourglass figure. "But somethin' else. You ain't never seen red hair until you see that broad's red hair! *Flamin'* red! An' hangin' all the way down to her shoulders."

"Did he pick her up here, or—"

"How could I tell? The *impression* I got was that they *met* here, that he knew she was comin', she knew he was comin'. I'm sure that's the way it was after the first time."

Kennelly took a sip of the beer Rudy had pushed toward him. "If I remember, you got no back door," he said.

"We got a *locked* back door. Otherwise, if you got two guys in the men's room, the third guy who comes along will go out the back and take a leak on the ground. We got a constant fight between the fire department and the health department. The fire guys want us to keep an open back door all the time, in case of emergency. The health guys don't want piss all over the ground out back. Puts us between a rock and

a— We choose to keep the door locked. You can't go out and take a leak in the alley. Not from here."

"Then if the scary guy and the redhead left together—"

"They went out the front door, to the street. Which means the guy didn't go out in the alley from here and get shot."

When Mrs. Roosevelt returned to the family quarters of the White House, she could hear music from the President's bedroom. She recognized the notes of a Chopin nocturne, though she was not sure just which one. She might have knocked on his door and stopped in to say goodnight, but she knew Missy had to be there—Missy changed the records as they played— and the First Lady's goodnight could only be an interruption of what was for the President a pleasant, relaxing hour. She went on to her own rooms.

She stood at a window and stared at the Ellipse. Wet snow now hung precariously from the trees, and blobs of it fell heavily, knocking more from lower limbs before it reached the ground. By morning there would be little left of the snowfall. The ground would be dark and soggy. She remembered times at Hyde Park when snow had lain on the ground for as long as two months without melting.

She sat down at the breakfront desk in her study and wrote a letter to her son Elliott. Part of what she said was—

I trust that your attempt to change your father's mind in the matter of the airmail contracts has been a learning experience. I learned long ago never to say to him that he has made a mistake or that to take a certain course *would be* a mistake. It is far better to suggest to him that he might consider alternative courses that possibly could achieve his purposes without certain disadvantages that may follow on the course he has taken or appears about to take.

Rereading these lines, she realized that her words were unlikely to have much impact on her son. Alice Roosevelt Longworth, the feisty daughter of President Theodore Roosevelt, had a way of saying things crisply, and her judgment of Elliott was that "Elliott is a naughty boy."

Kennelly decided to visit one more joint. Frankie One had been barhopping on K Street, for sure. He had not been seen in the company of Jessica Dee. On the other hand, he apparently had been with a striking redhead. Well . . . Andrea Alphand was described as a striking redhead with long hair. It would not be a waste of time to pursue the redhead as a line of inquiry.

The third bar was called Capitol K. It was one of very few bars in Washington where the races mixed. A few colored people, not many, crossed K Street and

mingled cautiously with the predominantly white crowd in Capitol K. Drinks were significantly more expensive on the north side of the street than they were on the south, and those Negroes who ventured over to Capitol K either were descendants of slaves and members of families who had lived for many decades in the city and had attained middle-class status, or crossed the street as a daring adventure. Most of the whites in the bar ignored them. Some engaged them in conversation—another sort of daring adventure.

A degree of tension always prevailed in Capitol K, and the police paid it special attention.

The K in Capitol K did not stand for the street name, as most people supposed, but for Kendall; the place was owned by Matty Kendall. Matty did not tend bar but hurried behind the bar when he saw Kennelly come in.

Matty was a fat and jovial man whose effeminacy of manner led to certain rumors about him. He carried a sap in his hip pocket, and the police, arriving to break up a fight, often found the combatants stretched out on the floor and waiting to be picked up.

His saloon was business-like. Matty had functioned throughout the Prohibition years, and the zinc bar sloped to the *rear* and into a gutter like an eaves trough. In the event of a raid, patrons had simply poured their drinks on the bar, the alcohol ran down to the gutter and was sluiced away by running water.

Other jets of water had rinsed the bar itself. Barrels of beer had descended into the cellar on dumbwaiters. Bottles of gin and whisky had been whisked away by the bartenders. After six raids Matty had never received a citation.

"Ed," said Matty in his high-pitched voice. "Something special." He did not offer Kennelly a beer but a double shot of single-malt Scotch and a tumbler of water. "To what do I owe the honor?"

Kennelly handed him the morgue photo of Frankie One.

"Vito Francione," said Matty.

"You recognize him?"

"How could I not? The story was in the newspapers that the body of Vito Francione, also known as Frankie One, was found in the alley behind my bar."

"Did he come in here?"

Matty nodded. "I suppose three or four times, maybe five. Obnoxious bastard."

"Did he meet a woman here?"

"Did he ever! The most gorgeous redhead you ever saw."

"Not a little blond?"

"No little blond."

"Was the redhead with him every time he came?"

"No. And she wasn't *with* him. They met here. I figure she was with him twice."

"Did she leave with him the night he went out your back door and was shot in the alley?"

Matty shook his head. "That, I cannot say, Sir. I didn't see them leave together. They could have."

Kennelly swallowed half of the Scotch Matty had poured him. "Ahh!" he said appreciatively. "First-class stuff, Matty."

"The best," said Matty.

"Uhh . . . gentlemen?" A man next to them at the bar sought their attention. "Gentlemen, I try not to listen to other people's conversations, but I couldn't help overhear what you've just been saying. You speak of a redhead meeting a man here. I saw them. Matty, you should *know* who the lady is."

"How would I know?"

The man looked at Kennelly and nodded. "Flaming red hair—long, smooth, glorious. In this decade when nearly every woman marcels or frizzes her hair, to see hair hanging free to the shoulders is a rare privilege. And *red*, red like that! My God, gentlemen! I'd know her anywhere. And so do you, if you think about it."

"Tell us what we are supposed to know," said Kennelly brusquely.

The man laughed. "The star of the Gayety Theater all this month! She dances—strips—under the stage name Blaze Flame. God knows what her real name is."

VIII

FOR THE SECOND TIME in two weeks, the First Lady was ushered incognito to an interview with a prisoner in the district jail. The striptease dancer Blaze Flame was not tearful at being in jail; she was furious. She was handcuffed to the chair, as Jessica had been, in Kennelly's office, and met with the First Lady alone.

She did not recognize Mrs. Roosevelt and took her for a woman detective. "I *have done nothing!*" she complained. "What am I supposed to have done? They haven't even *said.*"

Blaze Flame was a dramatically striking woman, beyond question. Her red hair was as had been described: copper-red and smooth and long. She was of medium height and possessed a spectacular figure, visible even through a loose gray cotton dress: the jail uniform. Her face and arms were freckled. Kennelly had shown photographs of Blaze wearing the heavy

makeup of a burlesque performer. The First Lady thought she was prettier without it.

"I have shows to do tonight. I can't afford to sit around in here. If you've got a charge against me, tell me what it is and let me get a lawyer. I have a right to know."

"Lieutenant Kennelly tells me you are charged with indecent exposure," said Mrs. Roosevelt.

"Indecent . . . ! I was no more naked last night than I've been any night since I came to Washington, and they never arrested me before. Anyway . . . a fifty-dollar fine. I'll pay it!"

Kennelly had told the First Lady that he would have to release Blaze Flame by mid-morning. The manager of the Gayety Theater had already come by and offered to pay her fine. Kennelly did not have enough against her to charge her with murder. But he wanted Mrs. Roosevelt to talk with her. He wondered if the woman might be enough impressed to say something unguarded.

"I believe the charge against you will be dropped shortly, Miss Flame. You will be released before noon. It will expedite the matter if you will answer a few questions."

Blaze Flame shrugged. "You wouldn't have a cigarette, would you?" she asked.

Mrs. Roosevelt opened Kennelly's desk drawer, where she knew he kept his Luckies. She shook out a cigarette and handed it to the young woman, then lit a match and held the fire up. Blaze Flame leaned forward, holding the cigarette between her lips and between two fingers of her free right hand.

"You were arrested because the police want to ask you some questions about Mr. Sargent Peavy."

"So the lieutenant said. Peavy's the fella that got killed last week. Well, I never met him. I *told* the lieutenant I never met him. He asked me about a man called Vito Francione or Frankie One. I never even *heard* of him."

"Where were you on the evening of Tuesday, February twelfth?"

"He asked me that, too. I was at the Gayety, doing my act. And that's where I was the night this Francione guy was killed. That's where I am six nights a week. We're closed on Sundays. I'm on four times a day, a matinee and three evening shows."

"Have you ever performed in Boston, Miss Blaze?"

"Boston, Providence, New Haven, New York, Philly, Baltimore, Washington, and Richmond. Then back to Boston again."

"Where are you from? I mean, where is your home?"

Blaze Flame drew deeply on her cigarette. "Cleveland," she said. "I started out on a different circuit—

Cleveland, Columbus, Cincinnati, Dayton, Akron, To-
ledo, Detroit, Pittsburgh." As she let a thick white
cloud of smoke roll out of her mouth and down over
her chin, she fixed a stare on the First Lady. "Wait a
minute," she said. "You're not some woman cop.
You're . . . *Jesus Christ, you're Mrs. Roosevelt!*"

"I am indeed . . . though I would be grateful if we
could keep it quiet that I came to see you."

"My God! The only other *famous* person that ever
came to see me was dear old Justice Oliver Wendell
Holmes, who used to come to the Gayety every time
the show changed. I understand he's very poorly now."

"Yes. I'm afraid so. Well . . . Since you have discovered my identity, would you mind telling me your real
name?"

Blaze Flame took another drag on her cigarette.
"Alexandra Zaferakes," she said. "My family is Greek.
My father works in a steel mill in Cleveland. I've had
to make my own living since I was sixteen. Understand, I'm not ashamed of what I do. But my family
would rather it was something else."

"I'm afraid you have been held an hour longer than
you otherwise might have been, in order that I might
get to meet you and talk with you. I'll suggest to Lieutenant Kennelly that you be released now."

"Kennelly is a typical cop. He locked me up over-
night so as to pressure me. To scare me. Same reason
for the handcuffs. I don't scare so easy. I've been a

stripper sixteen years, and I've been in and out of a lot of jails . . . Say, they don't really think I had anything to do with those two murders, do they?"

"A woman with long red hair is a suspect," said Mrs. Roosevelt. "There aren't many like you, Miss Zaferakes."

"Well, I had nothing to do with any murders."

"I'm inclined to believe her," Mrs. Roosevelt said to Kennelly when Blaze Flame had been sent back to the jail to pick up her things and be released.

"Oh, so am I," he admitted. "But her alibi is not airtight. She strips three times a night: at about eight, about ten, and about midnight. For the two hours in between, while the other strippers and the comics are working, she doesn't usually just sit backstage and wait. She goes out, sometimes to a bar for a beer, sometimes nobody knows where. She could have shot Peavy in Georgetown and been at the theater in time for her eight o'clock performance. She could have gone to K Street, met with Frankie One, and come back, all inside her two-hour break."

"She's not a crude woman by any means," said Mrs. Roosevelt. "Even so, it is difficult for me to imagine Sargent Peavy . . . Well, you know."

"Hard to think he'd fall for her," said Kennelly. "Hard to think he'd fall for a stripteaser. Not in character for him."

"Yes. I shouldn't think she would appeal to him. Which . . . uh . . . reminds me of a question that's been turning in my mind. When, uh, she does her *striptease* dance, just how much of her clothing does she remove?"

Kennelly rubbed his cheek. "Uh . . . well . . . When she is finished with her dance, her act— Let me put it this way. Uh . . . she is, uh, really a redhead. Her hair is not dyed."

"Oh, my!"

"Just for a second as she leaves the stage and the lights go out."

"And that is what Mr. Justice Holmes went to see?"

"All the years he was in Washington, until he grew too ill to go out, he went every time the show changed. He went to the old Howard Theater in Boston, before he came to Washington."

"I suppose other prominent men attend the performances."

"You may be sure of it, Ma'am."

"Well . . . Another question. Have you seen her performance?"

"Yes, I have."

"If she takes off all her clothes, wouldn't that reveal the wound we think the person who killed Mr. Francione suffered?"

Kennelly grinned. "I haven't seen her since Frankie One was killed. I guess I'll have to check that out."

. . .

Back in her office, Mrs. Roosevelt scanned the corre-
spondence. Tommy Thompson divided it into three
files—letters that raised some serious issue to which
the First Lady might decide to give her attention, com-
plimentary letters that deserved a form answer, and
what Tommy called the "hickory" letters, hickory
meaning hickory nuts. Sometimes Mrs. Roosevelt read
the hickory file, just for amusement, for relief of tension. One letter this morning gave her a smile—

PROSPERITY CLUB—IN GOD WE TRUST
Dear Honest Citizen,
    Hear is your chance to earn thousands of dol-
lars, from the investment of just a few cents! It is
eazy, so just read the instructions below and follow them.
    Below is a list of five names. Please send a dime
to the name at the top of the list. Cross out that
name and write your own at the bottom. Then
make five copies of this letter and send them to
five frends. Ask each frend to do the same. Soon
your name will be at the top of all the lists your
frend and your frends frends send out, and you
will begin to receive your dimes! If everyone is
honest and sends out one dime each, you will receive $1,562.50!
    Do the arithmetic yourself and see how it

works. The first letter in the chain produces 25, the second 125, the third 625, the fourth 3,125, and the fifth 15,625! By then <u>your</u> name will be at the top of the list, and <u>your</u> will get the $1,562.50!

Of course, it depends on all the people who get the letters sending out their letters in turn and not breaking the chain. <u>Breaking the chain has been proved to bring horrible bad luck!</u> A man in Illinois that broke the chain had his tractor upset on him and crush him. A woman in Iowa broke the chain and was soon blinded in a litening strike.

The best of luck and prosperity to you, dear frend. Send your letters and plan on how you will spend your dimes.

This was the third such letter Mrs. Roosevelt had received. The President had received at least ten. The chain-letter craze that had begun that winter had swamped post offices with letters. Postmaster General Farley had warned that chain letters were illegal, but that had not stopped the craze. Everyone received the letters. Countless thousands responded to them. It seemed that no one saw the fallacy in this get-rich-quick scheme. One-dollar, two-dollar, and three-dollar letters were also in circulation.

Mrs. Roosevelt smiled and tossed the letter in the trash, so risking having a tractor turn over on her or being struck by lightning.

Just after noon she received a call from Kennelly—
"Something a little odd," he said. "Letitia Peavy
returned from Massachusetts on schedule, then immediately disappeared. We've been keeping a kind of
eye on her, you know. She taught her classes on Tuesday but did not go home Tuesday night. She missed
her classes Wednesday and this morning. I'm more
than a little curious."

"As am I," said Mrs. Roosevelt.

"Well . . . I thought you would want to know."

"Indeed."

The First Lady telephoned her friend Elinor Morgenthau and told her what Kennelly had reported. "I
believe you said she has an inamorato: a man in uniform."

"If so," said Elinor Morgenthau, "she may have felt
free to slip away somewhere with him." She laughed
a tinkling little laugh. "After all, her husband has been
dead more than a week. She buried him Sunday."

Kennelly took a more ominous view of the disappear-
ance of Letitia Peavy. Her husband, after all, had been
murdered. Now *she* was missing. In his judgment, it
was adequate reason to take a look inside the Georgetown house. He saw no reason to get a warrant. If he
found anything significant inside the house, he would
get a search warrant and come back to seize it.

The mail was in the box, the newspapers on the

stoop. She had not been at home since Tuesday. Even so, he rang the doorbell and waited a minute or so. Then he used a skeleton key and entered the Peavy home.

He came to a quick conclusion: that when she left, probably on Tuesday morning, Letitia Peavy had not meant to return immediately. A woman who meant to come back that evening would almost surely have left her morning coffee cup on a kitchen counter or in the sink. She might have left the Tuesday-morning newspaper on the kitchen table. This house was too tidy. It was a house to which she had not meant to return Tuesday evening.

Or maybe—

He went upstairs to the bedroom where Sargent Peavy had been found dead on the floor. The rug had been taken away, and the floor was bare. He opened the door and looked into the bedroom closet. He looked through the other closet on the second floor. In that closet he saw a Gladstone bag: a man's suitcase. Nowhere did he see a woman's suitcase.

Had Letitia Peavy absquatulated?

Sargent Peavy's clothes remained neatly hanging in the two closets. Hers were there, too, but it seemed some were missing. Kennelly could not judge. How many dresses should a woman have?

He went through the dresser drawers. Letitia Peavy, it appeared, had abandoned bloomers and was

wearing the new ladies' French step-ins, called pant-ies. They covered her legs less than halfway from hip to knee. Not long ago he would have taken that as a statement about her morals. No more. The world had changed.

She wore silk. Her panties, slips, and teddies were all silk.

In the bathroom he found two one-dozen packages of rubber prophylactics. Well . . . a husband and wife would have them, unless they wanted children.

Nothing suggested anything. Until he looked into a handbag and saw a book of paper matches imprinted "Hotel Thayer." He had never heard of a hotel called Thayer and wondered where it might be. It was not in the Washington area.

The Peavys' car, a royal-blue 1930 Oldsmobile four-door, was in the garage behind the house.

Kennelly wondered if Letitia Peavy had gone to Ho-tel Thayer for a tryst. She was rumored to have a lover. If she did, she would have been anxious to see him—and anxious not to be seen seeing him.

Kennelly reported to Mrs. Roosevelt. She was about to board the presidential train for New York and then up the Hudson to Hyde Park. Tomorrow was Wash-ington's Birthday, and government offices would be closed. The President had decided to take a long week-end at his home on the Hudson.

"Yes, I do know where The Thayer is. It's at West Point. Do you think there is any real possibility that Mrs. Peavy is there? I can readily find out. It is only a short drive."

The presidential train was called POTUS, meaning President of the United States. The President boarded it at the Treasury Department where there was a loading facility that allowed him to be put aboard in his wheelchair with minimal inconvenience. The presidential car, once named the Ferdinand Magellan and now unnamed, was painted kelly green and was armored and extremely heavy. Another car carried the Secret Service contingent that followed a president everywhere and the special communications equipment that kept him in touch with the White House. Another was provided for the press. The steam locomotive strained to get the presidential train moving. The drive wheels spun on the tracks and shot sparks.

POTUS left Washington on the tracks of the Baltimore & Ohio Railroad and switched to the New York Central in the New York City marshaling yards. Because the swaying and pitching of a railroad car caused the President pain in his lower back, POTUS never traveled more than twenty-five or thirty miles an hour. This disrupted traffic on the railroads, and the Pennsylvania's reluctance in this respect caused the President to prefer the B & O.

Ferdinand Magellan—still so called although the

name had been painted over on its sides—was furnished with comfortable armchairs, a bath and bedroom of course, and a galley in which meals were prepared during a presidential journey.

Besides the President and Mrs. Roosevelt, Missy LeHand and Dr. McIntire were aboard.

With the train moving slowly, the President relaxed. Moving north, he saw the snow that had all but melted in Washington lay more heavily in Maryland and New Jersey.

"It's going to be beautiful up in the valley," he said, meaning the Hudson Valley. "I've always loved snow."

"We can perhaps have a rig hooked up and go for a sleigh ride," said Mrs. Roosevelt.

"Yes . . . I would like that."

He spoke listlessly. His thoughts were somewhere else. She could guess where: on his ice boat, on his skis, on his snowshoes, all of which had been lovingly preserved by his mother and were stored at Hyde Park. She almost never heard a note of sorrow in his voice, but she heard it now. And she knew that any effort she made to comfort him would be futile. She was awkward about things like that and always had been. Missy was better. Thank God for Missy!

"Well, how goes the Hawkshawing, Babs?" the President asked. Hawkshaw was the name of a Sherlock Holmes–type detective, known chiefly in 1935 as the subject of a comic strip.

"Apart from the fact that Letitia Peavy is missing, it is going rather well."

"Missing? What do you mean, missing?"

"Just that. She returned from Boston after burying her husband, taught her classes one day, then . . . disappeared."

"I have to suspect, Babs, that the elusive Mrs. Peavy is somewhere finding comfort," said the President.

"Either that or she murdered her husband and has gone on the lam," said Missy. "I hope the police are checking the ship lines."

"It makes things look," said the President, "a little more hopeful for your friend Jessica Dee."

The Thayer is the hotel for West Point. It looks like West Point. A huge, stone, Gothic structure with the architectural features of a medieval fort, it perfectly complements the main structures of the United States Military Academy. Never called the Thayer Hotel or Hotel Thayer, it is simply The Thayer: dignified and elegant. A landmark.

Mrs. Roosevelt sent word ahead that she would be driving over from Hyde Park on Friday and would like to meet with the manager. She allowed herself to be driven by a Secret Service agent, yet tried to be as inconspicuous as possible.

The manager was named Frank Dittoe: a hotel

manager who had earned a distinguished reputation in other hotels in Europe and America before being employed to manage The Thayer. He received the First Lady in a small private meeting room, where they could sit and enjoy the long view of the Hudson and Constitution Island. At eleven o'clock he offered glasses of Tio Pepe, an exquisite dry sherry Mrs. Roosevelt knew and appreciated. With the sherry he offered crumbled bits of Stilton cheese and tiny wafers.

"I regret," said Mrs. Roosevelt, "that I have never enjoyed the hospitality of The Thayer. I have heard of it since— Since when, Mr. Dittoe?"

"It was built in 1926," said Dittoe. He was a compact Italianate man with a swarthy complexion, a faultless manly face, and handsomely tailored clothes. "From the outset it has been meant to be . . . How shall I say? The epitome of elegance with dignity."

"I have not been a guest for only one reason. Hyde Park is—"

"Yes. Too close. But allow us sometime—"

"I certainly shall. And the President, too. But I have come today to ask a question, Mr. Dittoe."

"Any question I can answer, dear lady."

"Are you aware of the name Peavy? Sargent Peavy, who was murdered last week, or his wife Letitia Peavy?"

Dittoe nodded. "I have heard the name."

"Is Mrs. Peavy a guest in the hotel at the present

time? Has she been in the past few days?"

Dittoe smiled but shook his head. "My dear, dear lady," he said. "You must understand that, as a professional hotelier, I cannot divulge that kind of information. Indeed, if I were to be asked by the press if I had met with *you* this morning, it is a matter I would not divulge."

"Can you tell me if she has *ever* been a guest here?"

His smile broadened. "The identities of my guests must always remain confidential. If they wish to say they were here, they say they were here. I never disclose that information."

"If the police were to ask to read your registers, would they find her name?"

"I cannot say what names they would find, Madam."

Mrs. Roosevelt smiled broadly. "Mr. Dittoe, you are a credit to your profession. But, all without so intending, you have answered my question. If Mrs. Peavy had never been a guest here, you could simply have said so. You did not escape the question with that simple denial. So . . . she was here . . . sometime."

He nodded gracefully. "As you wish."

"The police fear she is dead, Mr. Dittoe."

"My dear lady, I can tell you this much—Mrs. Peavy is not dead. I am not betraying a confidence when I say that much."

IX

THE HUDSON VALLEY, UNDER six inches of snow, was glittering and refreshing as always: a welcome relief from Washington. The First Lady needed another kind of relief when she went to Hyde Park: relief from her domineering mother-in-law, Sara Roosevelt. To that end she had urged her husband, years before he became President of the United States, to give her a plot of land on the Hyde Park estate and build for her a cottage of her own. Her close friends Nancy Cook and Marion Dickerman lived in the cottage, which she called Val-Kill for the stream, or kill in Dutch, that ran through the property; and whenever she came to Hyde Park Mrs. Roosevelt spent as much time as she could at Val-Kill.

Her mother-in-law called the cottage a shack.

Val-Kill was not large, and it was not elegant, but it was her own; it was her home as the big house near the river never could be. On the second floor of the

big house, the President slept in an elegant bedroom suite with fireplace and its own bathroom. Mrs. Sara Roosevelt slept in a similar suite. Mrs. Eleanor Roosevelt slept in a small bedroom with no fireplace and had to use a bathroom shared with several other bedrooms.

Contrary to what most Americans thought, the Roosevelt home at Hyde Park was not a mansion. In fact, had been a frame farmhouse for many years, and it wasn't until after the death of the President's father that FDR had encouraged his mother to remodel it extensively. It was only then that the stucco façade had replaced the clapboards and the columned porch had been added, also with two wings to give it more rooms. The house was comfortable, but it was not one of the great Hudson River mansions.

Mrs. Roosevelt had dinner that Friday evening with the President and his mother, and as soon as she politely could she drove up the hill a mile and a half to Val-Kill.

Ed Kennelly had a couple of ideas. He went to the burlesque house for the matinee.

He knew the manager of the Gayety, had known him since the days when he was a beat cop and had sometimes slipped into the theater and stood in the back as if he were monitoring the performance to be

sure the strippers did not go too far—though he actually did it to get warm.

The world had changed. Now the strippers were
allowed to go too far. And some of the jokes . . .

Baggy-pants comic approaches straight man
standing before the curtain. "My, that's a pretty
girl across the street!"

"I know. I've just been scrutinizing her."

"You was over dere?"

"No, I scrutinized her from here."

"You're right here, an' she's over dere . . . an'
you *scrutinized* her? From here? All da way
across da street?"

"Of course."

"Wow! Dis I gotta see! What you do with it between scrutinizes, roll it up like a garden hose?"

The theater manager was Luke Runkel, a short
bald man with a placid face. He and Kennelly stood at
the rear of the theater so Kennelly could watch the
show while they talked. The lesser dancers were per-
forming, getting cheers and cries of "Take it off!"

"Take a look at the photo, Luke," said Kennelly.
He showed the morgue shot of Frankie One.

"Who's the stiff?"

"Question is, did you ever see him in here?"

Runkel turned down the corners of his mouth and

shrugged. "Thousands of guys come in here."

"Camel overcoat with white buttons. Spats on his shoes."

"Yeah?"

"Yeah. The town's not full of guys like that."

Runkel nodded. "Okay. Your morgue shot doesn't show any of that—meaning how he dressed. I saw the guy once or twice, sure. Yeah, he was in here."

"Next question. Did he come to see the show, or did he meet with somebody?"

"I wouldn't know that. I didn't see him meet with anybody, talk with anybody. But I might not see. I'm back in the office most of the time."

"Like, he didn't take one of the girls out between shows?"

"My girls do that, they're outa here. I got a strict rule: the show it, they don't sell it."

"I mean for a drink, just for a drink or a sandwich."

"I couldn't say."

"How long has Blaze Flame been here?"

"Two weeks, about. She'll be here another two weeks. She plays here a month every year. Very popular."

Kennelly stayed to see Blaze Flame's strip. She had no wound.

Next, Kennelly went to Jessica Dee's apartment. He rang and rang. Jessica was not there, so he let himself in and searched the place. As when he searched

the Peavy home, he saw no need for a warrant. If he found nothing, the young woman didn't have to know he'd been there. If he found something useful, there would be time enough to ask for a search warrant.

He had seen the place before and knew that Jessica lived well—far too well for the receptionist-librarian at Covington & Burling or a staff aide to Huey Long. Her furniture was ordinary—it was a furnished apartment—but the prints on her walls were art, no sailing ship in the moonlight, no Currier & Ives calendar prints.

He went to see what he had not seen on the day when he and other officers had conducted a perfunctory search. Other detectives made jokes about what they called his predilection for pawing through women's underwear, but Kennelly had solved important cases by looking into the drawers where men and women kept their private garments. Apart from learning something about who they were by what they wore, he had learned that people liked to hide things among their underclothes, apparently with the notion that detectives and burglars would be too embarrassed to search there.

Kennelly wasn't embarrassed. In Jessica's bureau he found delicate silk things, briefer and more expensive than Letitia Peavy's. She wore what they called tap panties, also lace-trimmed teddies. Her nightgowns had sheer panels in places where modesty

would have dictated opaque silk; they had been designed to display, not to conceal, things she might have been expected to conceal.

The labels, he thought, might tell him something. He took out a small notebook and wrote down the names from the labels in her intimate clothes. Most of the names were meaningless to him. One name did suggest something. He wasn't sure what the name meant, but he decided to bring it to the attention of Mrs. Roosevelt. Some of the young lady's scanties had been purchased in a store called Filene's. He was reasonably certain there was no such store in Washington. But the name was familiar. Where, then, might there be a store called Filene's?

He had closed the last drawer in Jessica Dee's bureau when he stiffened at sounds he heard. A key turned in the lock on the front door. A tinkling laugh sounded through the apartment. A man said something. She had come home! And she wasn't alone!

He was a police officer. But he was in a young woman's apartment without a warrant—and this was a young woman with influential friends; the man with her might be Senator Huey Long! The situation was dangerous for him. It was also ridiculous. Not only was he in her apartment, he was in her bedroom! Kennelly glanced at the bedroom window. He could not open it, slide through, and drop to the ground outside before—

"I'll slip into something more comfortable," said Jessica Dee with an insinuating laugh.

"I'll pour us a couple of drinks," said the man.

Seeing no choice, Kennelly made the ridiculous situation even worse. He rushed into her closet and closed the door. It could have been stupider only if he had crawled under her bed.

Surely she would open the closet and hang up her dress! And she did. He pressed himself as far back as he could in one corner. Laughing and talking to the man in the kitchen, she grabbed a hanger and carelessly hung her dress on it, without so much as glancing into the closet.

" 'Tis all I can do to help laughing at his accent. People laugh at mine. But that voice! All dripping with . . . What do Americans call it? Sorghum?"

"Molasses," said the man.

"Treacle." Jessica laughed.

She had not closed the door. From the corner of the closet, Kennelly had no good view of her, but he caught glimpses now and again that were enough to show him that she was taking off all her clothes and putting on one of the silk teddies from a bureau drawer. This one was pale-tea colored and trimmed with black lace. She shoved her feet into black, high-heel, patent-leather shoes and left the bedroom.

"What did you do with the photos?" Jessica asked.

"I left them in the cyahh," the man said.

"Not a good idea. We've got to keep those absolutely safe. I surely wouldn't want anybody to see them."

"They're under the seat. They're safe."

"I'm tempted to burn them," she said.

"No," the man said firmly.

"Well . . ."

"Nobody but us knows about them. I processed the film myself, you know."

"Your talents are endless. I've never known a man with so many talents."

Kennelly huddled in the closet, conscious both of the hazard and of how utterly preposterous his situation was. He wondered what photographs they were talking about, but then their conversation turned banal, and they began to exchange endearments. He wondered if they were so focused on each other that he might dare to sneak to the window. But no. If he could hear every word they said, they would hear him open the window.

"Hon . . ."

"Hmm?"

"Let's go to bed."

Kee-rist! They were going to bed, with him in the closet? What had been ridiculous and absurd was becoming insane! But he had no choice to huddle to one side of the closet and keep absolutely silent.

Kennelly was no voyeur. He did not *want* to see

what Jessica Dee and her man were going to do. In his closet corner, he stared determinedly at the hanging clothes and did not crane his neck to peer past them. He was embarrassed. But he could not help hearing them—

"*You bastard!*"

"Hey! Hey!"

"C'mon, c'mon. Don't play games . . ."

"Like that?"

"Yes, like that!"

They were never silent. When they didn't talk they grunted. Kennelly was profoundly uncomfortable. He had been married many years and was a father, but he had never guessed that a couple having sex could sound like this. Maybe he was old-fashioned. He was glad he was.

Eventually they were satisfied and fell silent. Then he smelled cigarette smoke.

After a while, she said, "I'm serious about the pictures. It's too much of a risk to leave them in the car."

"Alright. I'll take them home."

"And lock them—"

"In my safe."

"In your syfe. Aye. Right. In your syfe, an' only you can get in it, right?"

"Only I can get in it."

They did a second time what they'd gone to bed for. By now Kennelly began to feel the need to go to

the bathroom. My God! If they lolled in bed all evening, he'd—

"Let's go to dinner," the man said.

"Angus beef! What I'd give for a nice dinner of real Scottish beef!"

"It can be done," said the man. "I know a place. Of course, the beef is from Texas, but—"

"Well . . . A drink first."

Kennelly realized uncomfortably that they did not dress before they returned to the living room and sat without clothes while they had their drinks. But surely she would return and would rummage in the closet for a dress. Feeling more idiotic than he'd ever felt before in his life, he left the closet and crawled under the bed.

As it was both of them had to dress. The man sat on the bed, his legs and feet no more than twenty-four inches from Kennelly's face. Ludicrous though it was, he had made the right decision in crawling under the bed. Jessica Dee slipped hangars back and forth on the rod before she chose a frock for the evening. *Her* feet, as she drew on her stockings, were right in front of Kennelly.

"Any word from our lawyer, love?"

"Not a word."

"Well . . . If those pictures got in the wrong hands, there'd be a word."

"Quit worrying about it, Jessica. I promised you it's not going to happen, and it's not going to happen."

"I put all my trust in you."

When the couple at last left the apartment, Kennelly searched again, looking for a clue as to the identity of the man in whom she placed her trust, who would have photographs in his safe. He found nothing. They had indifferently left their filled prophylactics lying in an ashtray on the nightstand, but those were evidence of nothing.

Sara Roosevelt despised Louis McHenry Howe. She disliked his smoking and his drinking, his untidy clothes, his manners, his speech, his morals, and his close personal relationship with her son. She thought he was a bad influence on both Franklin and Eleanor. The truth was, she was jealous of him; she did not like anyone whom she perceived as having with Franklin a relationship as intimate as her own. Accordingly, Howe did not come to Hyde Park if he could avoid it. But he did arrive on Saturday afternoon. He would spend Sunday with the President and accompany him on the train ride back to Washington.

He was at the table for dinner Saturday evening— as were Sara, Eleanor, Missy, and the President.

Sara had managed to obtain some pheasants. She had seen to it that they had hung outdoors for four or five days to ripen, to gain that distinctive gamy flavor that game birds should have. These had been plucked and roasted at the perfect time, just as they began to

decompose and the carcasses had an aroma reminiscent of roasted coffee. By dinner they were delectable.

Eleanor could hardly eat. So far as she was concerned the pheasants had been allowed to spoil. It was a favorite joke of the President—but no laughing matter at all with Sara—that once Eleanor had ordered some birds put in the garbage just when they were reaching their ideal state. That had happened in Albany when FDR was governor. Sara could not conceal her scorn for her daughter-in-law's philistine tastes in food. Eleanor liked scrambled eggs, hot dogs, and tuna salad—which were for that reason banned from the Hyde Park pantry.

"We have to talk about Jessica Dee," said Louis Howe. He knew that, even though the President's mother detested him, he could talk about anything in her presence. She would never betray a confidence given to her son. "Huey's beginning to have second thoughts about our having placed her with him."

"I cannot and will not believe she murdered Sargent Peavy," said the First Lady.

"But there's some kind of major scandal in her background," said Howe. "*I* am the one who trusted her, after all."

"From what I hear," the President interjected with a grin, "she could charm the spots off a leopard. Did she charm you, Louie?"

Howe blew smoke in the air. Even though he was

eating a memorable meal, he kept a Sweet Caporal going, and at times his face was half obscured by the thick smoke hanging around it. "Damn right she did," he said.

"Just who is this young woman?" asked Sara Roosevelt.

"She's a refugee from Polish anti-Semitism," said the First Lady. "She was rescued from Poland and reared in Scotland."

"She's a Jewess?" asked Sara.

"Uh . . . she's Jewish," said Eleanor. She changed the subject. "I stopped over at The Thayer yesterday, Louie. Letitia Peavy returned from Boston on Monday, taught her Tuesday-morning classes, then disappeared. I had reason to suspect she might be at The Thayer, so I went over, met with the manager, and asked. He was quite cagey about it, but he in effect admitted that she had been there—if she was not in fact there at the moment. What do you make of that?"

"There have been rumors to the effect that Letitia sees a man. An element of the rumor is that he is a man in uniform. An army officer might well choose The Thayer for a trysting place."

"If he is prominent, I shouldn't think he would take his inamorata there. Surely he would be recognized at The Thayer."

"If he is a prominent officer, I imagine the hotel would go out of its way to keep his secret."

"All very gossipy," said the President. "Part of your Hawkshawing, I presume."

"If Jessica did not kill Sargent Peavy—establishing which will please Senator Long as well as ourselves—then somebody else did. That somebody could be Letitia."

"Spin me a scenario," said the President.

"Very well. Suppose there is a very serious love affair between Letitia and some army officer—which there very well could be, given all we know. Suppose . . . Oh, suppose a lot of things. Suppose that Mr. Peavy was threatening to expose the affair, which would ruin the officer's career. Suppose Letitia and the officer decided to kill him. Or suppose the officer alone decided to do it. An army officer might well be the expert marksman the killer had to be."

"This scenario fails to take two facts into account," said the President. "The newspaper story said that Peavy was stark naked. Why would he be stark naked in the presence of an army officer?"

"He was stark naked in the presence of his wife," said the First Lady. "Or he was stark naked in the presence of Andrea Alphand. And the officer came in and shot him. In either case, the officer fled with the woman: Letitia or Andrea."

"This doesn't explain the presence of Jessica's earring," Missy said skeptically.

"Unless Jessica did kill Sargent Peavy after all,"

said the First Lady, "obviously someone was at pains to make it look as though she did. It would have been a simple matter to break into her apartment and steal the earring."

"My!" Sara Roosevelt interjected. "Affairs, naked people, earrings . . . All this sounds very much like a parlor game."

"I'm afraid it's a good deal more than that, Mama," said the President.

"Well, sounds very much like a parlor game," Sara sniffed indignantly. "For myself, I'd rather play a nice board game like Parcheesi."

X

POTUS CHUGGED ITS WAY slowly south on the night of Sunday, February 24, and the early morning hours of February 25. The President retired early and enjoyed a long and restful night's sleep. He did not even awaken when the cars were switched from the New York Central to the Baltimore & Ohio in the New York City yards.

Mrs. Roosevelt, Louie, and Missy sat in comfortable chairs, chatted, and sipped—the First Lady sherry, the other two Scotch.

"Explain the Schechter case to me," Missy said to the other two. "It's so important to Effdee, and I have to confess I don't really understand it."

"The constitutionality of the National Recovery Act hangs on it," said Howe.

"Everything the President has tried to achieve since 1933 hangs on it," said Mrs. Roosevelt.

"Yes, but—"

"It's like a lot of other court cases," Howe interrupted. "The circumstances make a very important issue hang on a very minor case. The case, simply said,
is this— The Schechter brothers are in the business
of selling kosher chickens to New York people who
must have kosher poultry. That would seem like the
most noble and innocent of businesses: providing religious Jews with chickens that have been slaughtered
in accordance with religious law."

"One would certainly think so," said Mrs. Roosevelt. "But I have heard that there are problems."

Howe continued. "The problem is, the kosher
chicken business in New York City has become a
racket, involving falsified sales records and worse
things. The worst is that the dealers in kosher chickens slaughter and sell diseased chickens that are unfit
for human consumption. As you know, the National
Recovery Act authorizes the federal government to
sanction industrial codes. That is to say, industries
write sets of rules for themselves, and when they are
approved the NRA gives them the force of law. The
traders in live poultry wrote a set of rules for their
business. By selling sick chickens, the Schechter
Brothers violated those rules. The federal government
prosecuted."

"Which of course raises basic constitutional questions," said the First Lady.

"It raises two questions—first, can the Congress

delegate to an executive agency, the NRA, the power to make law, and, second, does the *federal* government constitutionally have the power to regulate the *intrastate* sale of poultry? If the Supreme Court says no, the entire National Recovery Act is unconstitutional."

"Effdee thinks we're going to lose," said Missy. "He's very worried about it."

"Looking at the antediluvian membership of the Supreme Court, I am afraid we are," said Howe. "Some of the justices seem determined to dismantle the entire New Deal."

"The President says they want to take us back to horse-and-buggy days," said Mrs. Roosevelt.

On Monday morning Mrs. Roosevelt telephoned Joseph Kennedy. "I should like to ask you, Mr. Kennedy, to use your contacts and resources in Boston to obtain some information for me. I should think you could obtain the information by telephone. Am I imposing?"

"Not at all. What can I find out for you?"

"As you may have read, a Bostonian by the name of Vito Francione, also known as Frankie One, was shot to death in an alley behind K Street during the evening of Tuesday of last week. I should like to know all there is to know about him."

"I can make some calls."

"I shall appreciate it. Now— You have told me

about the illicit activities of some of the officers and directors of the Cabot National Bank of Boston. Would there have been any connection between Mr. Francione and any of those men?"

"I . . . I would be surprised if there were any," said Kennedy. "But I can ask."

"Finally, where are those officers and directors now? Have any of them left Boston?"

"I can find out. I'll report back to you, probably this afternoon, after I make some calls."

Lieutenant Ed Kennelly sat in a booth in a delicatessen, across the table from Blaze Flame. She wore a tight, revealing red rayon dress, net stockings, and exaggerated high heels. She was outfitted to be seen by her admirers in the vicinity of the theater. Both were smoking, she with her cigarette in an amber holder. They had coffee in front of them, and sandwiches were coming.

"It's not wise to lie to the cops, Blaze."

"What lies you got in mind?"

"To start with, you told me you never met Frankie One, didn't know who he was. Well, I have an eyewitness who's ready to swear he saw you in the Capitol K Bar with Frankie. In fact, I got two witnesses, since the bartender will swear to it also."

"I don't care what they swear to. I never been in any bar called the Capitol K. In fact, I never been bar-

hoppin' on K Street. That's not my thing."

"Also, Frankie One was seen in the Gayety, more than once. More than once."

"Lots of guys come to the Gayety."

"They see the show," said Kennelly. "Then they don't come back until the show changes."

"You really think so? You've seen my act, Kennelly. You like to see it more than once? Some guys come and sit in the front rows night after night."

"Okay. Something else. You told me your father is a steel worker in Cleveland. That's not exactly true, is it?"

"Not exactly."

"Your old man did time for robbery and for assault and battery. He was charged with two murders."

"And acquitted," she said.

"And acquitted. But your brother wasn't. He died in the electric chair."

Blaze Flame thrust her hands across the table toward Kennelly. "You wanta lock the cuffs on me?" she asked bitterly, tearfully. "You wanta take me to the slammer again? Do you? Because my old man was a crook doesn't make me one. Because my brother was a murderer doesn't make me one."

"Why did you lie?"

"Wouldn't you?"

"You carrying a gun?"

"No, I'm not carrying a gun."

"You were arrested in Philadelphia last year for carrying a concealed weapon."

"And released. A girl like me can get attacked on the street, after dark. Some guys that see you on the stage think that gives them some kind of right to—"

"I'm gonna tell you something, Blaze," Kennelly interrupted sternly. "You got—what?—two more weeks in Washington. I hope to hell we get this Peavy case, and the Frankie case, settled by then. If we don't, I can't have you leavin' town. I don't want to lock you up, but I don't want to lose track of you."

"Man," she said, "there's no way you're gonna lose track of Blaze Flame. Wherever I go, people know I'm there."

Men like James Farley and Louis Howe were uncomfortably conscious that the President and Mrs. Roosevelt bore, to a considerable extent, reputations as Hudson Valley patricians—sometimes called patroons for their Dutch ancestry. A segment of American society supposed them to be aristocratic, "uppity." Farley and Howe made it a point to have them seen in the company of as wide a variety of Americans as possible. Since it was difficult for the President to spend much time with all the people those men would have liked for him to see, the responsibility fell on the First Lady.

Her visit from Shirley Temple last week had been

an example of Mrs. Roosevelt discharging this duty. Sometimes it was pleasant, as when she chatted with the tyke. Sometimes it was taxing, as when she visited poor people in their homes. She truly did not feel condescending but was conscious of how easily she might give that impression if she were not careful. At other times she had to try to distance herself from the enthusiasms of groups who fervently sought her endorsement of their causes. Sometimes the encounters verged on silly.

For lunch this Monday she was meeting with three of the famous Marx Brothers—Groucho, Harpo, and Chico—and the acclaimed Brooklyn Dodgers baseball pitcher, Van Lingle Mungo.

His unusual name alone would have made Mungo a fan favorite, but he was an outstanding pitcher with several important records to his credit. He had pitched 315 innings in the 1934 season. The Brooklyn Dodgers were known as "the zaniest team in baseball," and Van Lingle Mungo had a lot to do with that image.

Julius Marx, Groucho, would have preferred to omit his greasepaint mustache for a visit to the White House. But everyone involved in arranging the meeting with the First Lady insisted he must wear it—at least until the photographers were dismissed. Similarly, Arthur Marx, Harpo, would have left at home his curly blond wig; and Leonard, Chico, would have left his conical hat; but once again the patrons of the visit

demanded that the brothers appear in character.

Mrs. Roosevelt understood and was sympathetic. She posed with the brothers and the pitcher for the still and motion-picture cameras and fed Groucho straight lines to which he responded in character.

"Hello, Mr. Marx."

"Hello, hello, I must be going. I cannot stay. I cannot stay. I must be going."

"Welcome to the White House."

"Please. That's *my* line. I voted to get you here. Welcome to the White House!"

"Thank you, Mr. Marx. I am pleased to be here."

Before they sat down to lunch in the private dining room, from which all newspeople were strictly excluded for the occasion, Groucho was given time to wipe off his mustache, Chico abandoned his Italianate role, and Harpo began to talk.

Mungo had no reason to change character. He was a South Carolinian, twenty-four years old, and at six-feet-two the only person in the room who was taller than the First Lady. Of the macaroni salad that was the main course of the White House luncheon, he said shyly, "Y'all sure do eat elegant."

The three Marx brothers were subdued, once they were liberated from their roles.

"It is a great honor to be asked to lunch with the First Lady," said Groucho.

The First Lady spoke to Arthur—Harpo. "I arranged for a harp to be made available," she said. "I would be most grateful if you would play for us."

Harpo looked around the room and saw no harp. "I should be happy, but—"

"It is in the Oval Office," said Mrs. Roosevelt. "The President could not spare the time to join us for lunch, but he will be delighted to meet all of you and grateful if you would play for him, Mr. Marx."

Missy and Louie joined the President in the Oval Office when Harpo played. The President, cigarette holder atilt, nodded appreciatively as Harpo Marx, who had a real talent for the harp, played three classical selections. For two of them, Chico played a piano accompaniment. A White House photographer took pictures. The public, if they had ever seen those photographs, might not have recognized the Marx Brothers—though they might have recognized the lanky, bemused Van Lingle Mungo.

When she returned to her study and to some work laid out for her by Tommy, Mrs. Roosevelt found a message from Joseph Kennedy, who offered to stop by the White House later in the afternoon to report on what he had learned from his calls to Boston.

Mrs. Roosevelt asked him to stop by about four,

and she telephoned Stanlislaw Szczygiel and asked him to join them. She also called Ed Kennelly, but he was away from his office.

She received the two men in her study. She had uncovered the chalkboard on which she had made notes on the Peavy murder, some ten days ago.

(1) Jessica. But <u>why?</u> Cannot continue a love affair with a dead man. Heat of passion? But came with gun, gloves.

(2) Mrs. Peavy, out of jealousy over Jessica or another woman.

(3) Jessica's new lover. To get rid of a rival for Jessica's affections.

(4) Mr. Peavy's new lover, for whatever reason.

(5) The husband or lover of that woman, out of jealousy.

~~(6) None of the above but someone who had reason to oppose some policy Mr. Peavy was advocating at the Federal Reserve Board.~~

(6) Mrs. Peavy's lover.

(7) "Andrea Alphand"—who <u>may</u> be Miss Zaferakes (Blaze Flame).

(8) Mr. Francione, perhaps hired by someone at bank.

"I'm afraid my chalkboard has become something of a mess," said Mrs. Roosevelt.

"You can cross out your number eight," said Kennedy. "Frankie One was seen in Boston on the eleventh, twelfth, and thirteenth of the month."

"And Mr. Peavy was killed on the twelfth," said Mrs. Roosevelt. She rose and used her chalk to scratch through number eight.

"If not for his ironclad alibi, Frankie would have been a perfect suspect," said Kennedy. "He was a leg-breaker. He was used by the mob to collect loanshark loans and gambling debts. A thoroughly nasty sort of fellow. He may actually have been a hit man, too."

"A man hired to commit murder," Szczygiel explained to Mrs. Roosevelt.

She nodded. "Yes. I am familiar with the term."

"Is there any reason to suspect a connection between Mr. Francione and any of the officers and directors of the Cabot National Bank of Boston?"

"In other words, could one of the officers or directors of the bank have hired Frankie One to kill Peavy and so shut him up. Well . . . I like the guess, but nobody I talked to could imagine such a connection."

"A further question," said Mrs. Roosevelt, "is whether or not any of the officers or directors is missing?"

"The United States District Attorney in Boston asked the Boston police to assist his office by keeping an eye on the officers and directors. With two exceptions, they are all in Boston."

"The exceptions?"

"One vice president has disappeared entirely. The other exception is a vice president by the name of Charles Flaherty. He left Boston on February eleventh, the day before the murder. But he's not missing. We know where he is. He's here in Washington, staying at the Mayflower Hotel. He was in New York on the twelfth and came on down here on the fourteenth."

"In New York the evening the murder happened," mused Mrs. Roosevelt. "How convenient."

"He made some people nervous for about ten days in January, when he disappeared. But he came back to Boston. No one knows where he was."

"I have to believe the murderer was a woman," said Szczygiel. "What else explains Peavy's being found naked?"

"And with empty seminal vesicles," said Mrs. Roosevelt.

"I called a man I would as soon not talk to," said Kennedy. "I wouldn't want it known I did talk to him. He's known in Boston as 'the chief of chiefs.' That is to say, he's the head man of the New England mob, the way Luciano is head man in New York. I asked him to confide in me."

"And did he?"

"I asked him this—Suppose a man wanted another man killed, say in Washington. Who could he hire? Well, he named four or five hit men, mostly from Chi-

cago, one from Cleveland. He did not mention Frankie One."

"No women?" asked Mrs. Roosevelt.

"That's my point," said Kennedy. "I told him it was possible that Sargent Peavy had been killed by a woman, maybe a woman with red hair. 'Ah-ha!' he said. 'Yeah! Sure! From Los Angeles. Beverly Hill, she calls herself. One of the most effective and scary hitters in the world, I'm told. And the most expensive. They say she's got long red hair.' So—"

"So Andrea Alphand, also known as Beverly Hill, moves up on our list," said the First Lady. "It's fanciful but just fanciful enough perhaps to be true. And—" She smiled. "I *may* be able to give her two more names: Blaze Flame and Alexandra Zaferakes!"

"Blaze . . . ?"

"One more thing, Mr. Kennedy." She took from a drawer of her desk a photograph of the stripteaser. "Is that Andrea Alphand?"

Kennedy grinned and shook his head. "Well, I only saw her once, but I'm certain that's not Andrea Alphand."

Ed Kennelly, having received a message that the First Lady was trying to reach him, called as she was dressing to go out to dinner.

She told him what Kennedy had reported: that Frankie One had had a perfect alibi for the night of

Peavy's death and that there was a professional killer from Los Angeles who was a woman with red hair. Also, that Blaze Flame was not Andrea Alphand.

"Also, a vice president of the Cabot National Bank of Boston is living in the Mayflower Hotel. It might be well if you paid him a visit, Lieutenant. Don't you think?"

"I'll do that. Now I have a question for you, Mrs. Roosevelt. Don't ask me how I know, but Jessica Dee wears some very expensive lingerie. The labels in them say they came from a store called Filene's. Just where would that be? Do you know?"

"Assuredly. It's a very famous store. In Boston."

"So Jessica's fancy scanties come from Boston. I think that's kind of interesting, don't you?"

"It is suggestive," said Mrs. Roosevelt. "I am not aware that Jessica has ever been in Boston."

XI

BEFORE THEY FINISHED THEIR telephone conversation Monday evening, Mrs. Roosevelt suggested to Ed Kennelly that it might be a good idea if he were to go to the Mayflower Hotel and see what impression he could gain of the Boston banker Charles Flaherty. He stopped by the hotel about eight and learned that Flaherty was out. He hadn't *checked* out; he was just out, apparently for the evening. Kennelly decided to go back in the morning.

The Peavy murder was not the only case on his desk, and it was ten o'clock before he found time to delegate responsibilities and return to the Mayflower.

At the desk, Kennelly showed his shield and asked for a key to Flaherty's room. He was suspicious as to why this banker was spending so much time in Washington, and he resolved to surprise him and give him no time to think up answers to questions.

At the door to 814, he knocked to give the man a

moment's warning, then shoved the key in the lock and turned it.

He opened the door, and—

The body of a man clad in pajamas, a robe and slippers lay face down on the floor. The back of his head had been blown off, and the room sprayed with blood and brain.

Kennelly stepped inside and closed the door. He went to the telephone and called headquarters.

After that he called Mrs. Roosevelt. "I don't yet know at what time he was shot, but it would be helpful if you could find out where Jessica Dee has been this morning."

"I will do so, Lieutenant. Please let me know what your investigation develops."

The room where the body lay was the parlor of a suite. A room-service breakfast tray with a half-eaten breakfast of bacon and eggs sat on a coffee table before the couch. Kennelly called room service.

"This is Lieutenant Edward Kennelly, Washington police. I'm in Room 814. I need to know when breakfast was ordered for this room and when it was delivered."

"I'll see if I can find out right quick, Suh."

Kennelly waited impatiently until finally a different voice came on the line. "This 'ere's Sid. Ah took the breakfast up to 814. You say you wanta know what time that wuz? Well, it wuz about nine-thirty."

"Did you see the man in the room?" Was he alone?

"Yassuh. Mr. Flaherty alone. He sign the check and gimme a quarter, like every morning."

"Thank you, Sid."

Okay. Flaherty had been alive at half past nine. Sometime between then and Kennelly's arrival about a quarter after ten, someone had arrived here and shot the man.

Two uniformed officers were the first to arrive in response to Kennelly's call. He told them to start knocking on doors up and down the hall, to ask if anyone had heard the shot.

The hotel manager came next. "What a mess!" he exclaimed dolefully, looking at the gore splattered over carpet, furniture, and walls. "It will cost hundreds to clean this up."

Kennelly noticed a rubber glove lying in the gore. Looking around, he spotted another one under the coffee table.

All but two of the rooms along that corridor had been vacated. The guests had checked out. The manager called downstairs and got the checkout times.

Two of the rooms, 810 and 817 were still occupied. Kennelly went to talk to the occupants.

"Griffith is the name," said the bulky red-haired man in 817. "I'm an automobile dealer from Marietta, Ohio, in Washington to talk to my congressman. I

came in on the B&O last evening and will be going back late this afternoon."

"I have just one question, Mr. Griffith," Kennelly said. "Did you hear a shot fired this morning?"

"Why, no. No. I didn't hear any shot. Why?"

"The man in 814 was murdered between nine-thirty and a quarter after ten. The shot was fired from the hall or just in the doorway. It was a heavy-caliber pistol that would have made a big bang."

"My God! No, I didn't hear any shot. The only thing is . . . I did take a shower about that time. Maybe the water would have kept me from hearing."

Room 810 was also a suite. It was occupied by a couple who had registered as "Mr. & Mrs. Jack Mc-Coy." They had heard no shot. They had heard nothing unusual.

"Uh . . . uh, Lieutenant. Uh . . . will our names have to appear in the newspapers?"

Kennelly grinned. "No, Mr. McCoy, your name won't be in the newspapers."

"Well, you see—"

"I know," Kennelly interrupted. "I've known Millie for some time. Looks like you're doing okay, kiddo."

"You, too, Kennelly," she said. "You look fat and healthy."

"Let's leave that 'fat' part out," he said. "Did you explain to Mr. McCoy that the hotel knows you, too?"

"C'mon, Kennelly . . ."

"Actually, I admire your taste, Mr. McCoy. And I won't mention you to any reporters."

On the way back to 814 he told the uniformed officers to forget the names of the people in 810 and 817.

Another detective had arrived: Sergeant Leon Wenzel, a younger man than Kennelly who had little beat experience, became a detective within two years of arriving on the force. He had though, two years of college education and was well regarded. He had sandy hair and a handsome, freckled face.

He had picked up a spent cartridge, and it lay on the coffee table, on his handkerchief. "An automatic," said Wenzel. "It ejected its cartridge. It was lying there." He pointed at an ink mark he had made on the carpet to show where the cartridge had been. "Means the shot was fired inside, not through the door. Nine millimeter."

"No one heard the shot," Kennelly told Wenzel. "A silenced pistol. Sounds like a professional hit."

When the men from the medical examiner's office turned the body over, the job looked all the more like a professional hit. Flaherty had been killed with a single shot to the middle of his forehead.

"Just like Peavy," said Wenzel.

Using tongs, one of the medical examiners reached into the big hole in the back of Flaherty's head and pulled out a slug. He dropped it into a glassine envelope and handed it to Kennelly.

"Nine millimeter," said Wenzel. "It will match the cartridge. How much you want to bet it came from the same gun that killed Peavy and Frankie?"

"Ballistics," said Kennelly.

The body was covered but remained on the floor. Kennelly and Wenzel interrogated hotel personnel.

The chambermaid for that part of that floor was named Ruby Washington. She was a black woman, thirty-five years old, a little too plump but otherwise handsome. "I done got used to his habits," she said of Flaherty. "Couldn' clean up *his* room much before noon. Most mornin's it was the *lass* one."

"Did he ever have a woman in his room?" Wenzel asked.

"Well, now . . . how could I tell? I never seen no sign of it. He smoked a lot of cigars, drank a lot of whiskey—which is why he slep' so late, I figger."

As they talked, Wenzel prowled around the rooms, the parlor, bedroom, and bathroom.

"Ed . . . Look at this "

Kennelly went to the bedroom door and looked in. A brown leather valise lay open on the bed. It was empty.

"I wonder what was in there," said Wenzel.

"Leon! Come out of the bedroom. Walk around this way."

"What . . . ?"

"Ruby," said Kennelly. "When you clean this suite, do you run the vacuum cleaner?"

"Yassuh. Part of the job, specially when you cleanin' up after a man that spills cigar ashes all over."

"Well, come here. Look at this rug. What would you call those little marks?"

"Dems dents made by high-heel shoes . . . *stylish* high-heel shoes, that kind with what they call spike heels. They's bad for *new* rugs, what got a deep pile not yit wore down."

"When you vacuum, do marks like that disappear?"

"Dey *better!* Mistah *dee*tective, I got no job if I don't get rid of marks like that."

"So these marks had to be made since you last cleaned these rooms—say late yesterday morning."

She stared hard at the indentations. "Yassuh. An' mo'. Them ain't been walked over much. You walk back and forth over marks like that, dey gits shallower an' shallower."

"Have you see the valise before?" Wenzel asked.

"Yassuh. He kep' it in an odd place. Under de bed. I'd nudge it when I run the vacuum cleaner under dere."

"Did he have other luggage?"

"He had a suitcase in de closet. Leather. Nothin' cheap 'bout de man."

The suitcase proved to be empty. Planning to stay awhile, Flaherty had unloaded his suitcase into the bureau drawers. An expensive gold watch lay on the night table. A wallet containing more than a hundred fifty dollars lay on the bureau, together with other money in small bills and change. Kennelly pulled a five-dollar bill out of the untidy pile of money and handed it to Ruby Washington.

"The key here is, what was in that valise?" said Kennelly.

Early in the afternoon, the First Lady sat down to write a letter to her friend Lorena Hickock. Lorena had been a wire-service reporter, one of the first to be assigned to Eleanor Roosevelt, and they had developed a warm friendship. When Franklin Roosevelt became President, he appointed Lorena to travel around the country and inspect various projects for the relief of poverty. After Lorena and Eleanor had become accustomed to seeing each other nearly every day, these inspection trips meant they would be separated for weeks on end.

They called each other Hick and Mrs. Doaks—Mrs. Doaks being a name Mrs. Roosevelt had invented for herself, reflecting her wish to be an ordinary person not pursued every minute by reporters.

She wrote—

Dearest, dearest Hick,

How I miss you! How bleak life is without you! How I long to hold you in my arms and plant kisses on you!

On your eyes, dear Hick. On your mouth. On you everywhere!

The horrible rumors of a year or so ago seem to have been laid to rest. We may be indebted to Louie for that. How understanding the man is! How I laugh at myself when I recall how I disliked Louie at first. He understands, as Franklin does, how much I love you, and how I love you.

The letter was never mailed. She had not finished it when the telephone rang and Lorena was on the line.

"You will not believe it, my darling, but I am at *home! * Doak, *I flew!* I know you have done it, but I had not and— Oh, it makes no difference. I am home and dying to see you."

"See me you shall, dearest one. Tonight. Here. We shall dine. You will stay all night! Oh, Hick!"

The First Lady went to the Oval Office. Missy found a way to insert her between two of the President's appointments, and she went in to talk to him for a moment.

"Oh, Franklin! Hick is in Washington! She *flew* here from West Virginia! I want her to . . . I want her to be at your cocktail hour this evening."

"Of course. Be glad to see the old pig again."

"Franklin!"

"Well, she does carry a lot of flab."

"Franklin . . ."

The President grinned. "You make sure she is present for the evening 'at home.' And, uh . . . Do I have to raise the old subject?"

"No, Franklin. We will be circumspect."

"Babs . . . *I* know, and you know, and Louie and Missy know, and a lot of other people know . . . that the talk and gestures exchanged between you and Hick are expressions of enthusiastic friendship and no more. It's a way of expressing yourself that you learned in England—though where Hick learned it, I don't know. My mother talks the same way to her women friends, and where she learned it I don't know. It's old-fashioned, Babs. To this cynical generation that lives today, it suggests something you and Hick do not intend. All I ask is that you and Hick kiss and caress in private to your hearts' content. But not where others can see and hear."

Mrs. Roosevelt nodded and took a small handkerchief to wipe tears from her cheeks. "It's so *unnatural*, Franklin. I mean this goldfish-bowl life, in which one's every gesture is misinterpreted."

"I know."

"I love Hick. I love Louie. You love Missy. Does that have to mean that . . . ?"

"You bring the old girl to the 'at home,' " said the President. "I'll be glad to see her, all hundred-eighty pounds of her."

By the time Kennelly met with Mrs. Roosevelt late that afternoon at the White House, a ballistics test had confirmed that the shot that killed Flaherty had come from the same gun as had fired the shots into Peavy and Francione.

"I am pleased by one thing," said the First Lady. "Jessica Dee arrived at Senator Long's office this morning at eight-thirty and was seen there constantly until she left for lunch at noon."

"Don't ask me how I know this, but dear little Jessica is deeply concerned about certain photographs that she seems to think would destroy her if we saw them. You know, it is just possible that the gun that killed Peavy was passed to someone else to kill Frankie One, then to someone else to kill Flaherty."

"Isn't that a bit fanciful?"

"Jessica lied to us," said Kennelly. "I grant you that things look better for her, but I still want to know why she lied."

"Ed . . ." The First Lady paused and smiled, conscious that she had called Kennelly by his first name. "The evidence points to a professional killer, a hit man—or hit woman."

"Blaze Starr swears she was asleep in her hotel

room until almost eleven. She can't prove it, though."

"She has no bullet wound, you said."

"We could be off base on that," said Kennelly. "We may have put too much emphasis on a few drops of blood in an alley where spilling blood is not entirely uncommon."

"Letitia Peavy has returned, incidentally. The university takes the attitude that a woman whose husband was murdered is entitled to be a bit erratic for a while. But I should like to know with whom she stayed at The Thayer."

"One of two kinds of people," Kennelly suggested. "Either it was a prominent army officer who could count on the hotel to receive him secretly and keep his stay confidential, or it was someone who would never be recognized by the army types who go to that hotel."

"A married officer who did not want his wife to discover his relationship with Letitia Peavy . . ." mused Mrs. Roosevelt. She smiled slyly. "An officer with his marksmanship medal."

"Who got Peavy to take off his clothes before he shot him," said Kennelly. "I'm afraid it goes back to Andrea Alphand, who may or may not be Blaze Flame."

"Los Angeles," said the First Lady. "Don't I recall that Mr. Flaherty was missing from Boston for some ten days in January. Is it possible that he went to Los

Angeles and hired this variously named woman—"

Kennelly chuckled. " 'Beverly Hill,' " he said.

"—and hired her to come to Washington, form a relationship with Sargent Peavy, and kill him. One of the most feared hitters in America, your informant said."

Kennelly nodded. "Which doesn't explain Frankie One or Flaherty."

"Actually, it might explain the death of Mr. Flaherty," said Mrs. Roosevelt. "You said the killer of Mr. Flaherty took the time to go into his bedroom and find a valise under the bed. You saw the valise empty. What had the killer taken from it?"

"I see what you mean."

"*Money*. The hit person had not been paid. Or had not been paid in full. So the murderer—Beverly Hill if we may so call her—came to the Mayflower Hotel to demand the money. Possibly she had demanded it before and had been put off. This time she came determined to have the money or Mr. Flaherty's life."

"Or both," said Kennelly.

"Yes, I should think her preference would be both. She killed Mr. Flaherty, searched for and found the money, and—"

"And probably scrammed out of there within twenty minutes before I came to the door," said Kennelly.

"It was a close-run thing, I should judge."

· · ·

"Who's home?" The President issued his usual sum-
mons despite the fact he knew perfectly well who was
at home.

Only one person was invariably present, and that
was Missy LeHand. His faithful secretary was always
there. Besides Missy, Louie was there, also Harry the
Hop. The First Lady rarely came, but of course tonight
she was there, with her friend Hick. A surprise guest
was Jessica Dee. The First Lady had all but forgotten
how she came to know Jessica, but Louie had not forgotten, and he had invited her to the White House late
that afternoon to debrief her on what she had learned
in the past week from her job with the Kingfish.

Lorena Hickock was, as the President had suggested, a heavyset woman, though she did not weigh
nearly the hundred eighty pounds he had conjectured.
She was a dark-haired, open-faced woman with a
pleasant personality and conspicuous talent as a
writer.

It might have seemed that no two women could be
more different and less likely to appeal to each other
than the First Lady and her friend. Not only did Hick
enjoy her liquor and consume quantities of it, she also
smoked cigars. She was most emphatically not the
kind of lady that Eleanor Roosevelt had been brought
up to be and tried to be.

It was more likely that the President would enjoy

her, and enjoy her he did—a certain amount of her.

"Sister Hick," he said, "I've read some of your reports from around the country. Babs told me about the people who eat clay, but you've seen it."

"I have indeed, Mr. President. It is a pitiful sight. They've been doing it for generations. It is not of the Depression."

"It is in fact cultural," said Harry Hopkins. "African people have eaten clays for many centuries, and the practice was brought to America with the slaves, where it spread to the poor white population. It is not just a matter of eating dirt. The geophagists distinguish good dirt from bad dirt, and some of them travel many miles to find the nutritional dirt they want."

"Nutrition?"

"The clay is rich in certain minerals, and it is a prime source of it. Pregnant women in particular eat it."

"In some southern countries," said Hick, "twenty-five percent of the children in school eat clay. We could survey them. We had no way to survey their parents. But we can assume that twenty-five percent of adults also eat dirt."

"I' Scotland people eat oats," said Jessica, "which i' England is fed to horses. Or so said Samuel Johnson."

Mrs. Roosevelt, too, was anxious to turn the con-

versation away from geophagy and said, "We eat oats in America, too."

"No' really," said Jessica. "In America you put in so much water and milk that what you really eat is oats soup. You can break a tooth on Scots oatmeal."

The President laughed. "I was warned about you, Miss Dee," he said.

"Do the Kingfish for us, Jessica," said Louie Howe.

"Well . . . He was explaining to a visitor why he didn't join the army during the Great War." Everyone knew the story that Huey Long had been a notary public and claimed he was exempt from the draft because he was a state official. "He said, 'Ah di'nt go fat in France 'cause Ah wuzn't mad at nobody over thar.' "

While they all were laughing, Tommy Thompson came out from Mrs. Roosevelt's study and bent over her to whisper in her ear. "Lieutenant Kennelly is on the line."

The First Lady excused herself and went to take the call.

"Got an interesting little break this afternoon," Kennelly said. "You've noticed, I'm sure, that a certain number of lounge lizards hang out in the lobby of the Mayflower. Well, my boys' instructions were to talk to everyone who might have been in the lobby around nine, nine-thirty this morning. One of those loafers insists he saw a redheaded woman come in, go to the elevators and go up, then shortly come down. The el-

evator boy's shift had ended, but my man got his name, and we went to see him. He said, sure, he'd taken a striking redhead up to eight and brought her down ten minutes or so later."

"Miss Zaferakes?" asked Mrs. Roosevelt.

"Nope. I showed him a picture of Blaze, and he swears it wasn't her. And, of course, Kennedy said Blaze wasn't Andrea Alphand."

"What's the term for what you're going to do now, Ed? Put out an 'all-points bulletin' about Miss Alphand?"

"Something like that," said Kennelly dryly. "And . . . one thing more. The murder weapon is a Beretta, an Italian-made pistol, 1934 model. It fires what is called a nine-millimeter short cartridge. Very distinctive. There couldn't be many of them in the United States. The short cartridge doesn't make a big bang in the first place, and the 1934 Beretta lends itself to being silenced."

XII

WEDNESDAY MORNING MRS. ROOSEVELT telephoned Joseph Kennedy. "I am afraid I am becoming
a nuisance to you, Mr. Kennedy, but I am very much
interested in discovering who murdered Sargent
Peavy."

"As am I, Ma'am," said Kennedy. "As am I. Anything I can do, don't hesitate to ask."

"Well . . . The investigation focuses more and more
on a red-haired young woman. Reviewing, I realize
that it was from you that we got the name Andrea
Alphand and the information that Mr. Peavy was seeing her. Perhaps I should have asked you before, but
I wonder how certain you are that he *was* seeing her
and what you know about the nature of the relationship."

Kennedy paused significantly. "I . . . saw them together just one time. In fact, that is the only time I ever
saw Andrea. It was in a roadhouse on the Columbia

Pike, out in Virginia—called the Silver Moon. You know the sort of place. They have gambling and liquor, all very illegal. They also have rooms upstairs where— Well. You know. Anyway, I saw Sarge there with a redhead."

"Andrea Alphand."

"Andrea Alphand. I remember the evening vividly. The Moon is a place where lots of people go, but it's also a place where they don't care to be seen. If you think about it, what hazard is there in being seen there? If somebody says, 'I saw you at the Silver Moon,' you answer, 'Well, what were *you* doing there?' I've seen a number of prominent people there. In fact, that night Father Coughlin was there."

"The radio priest, from Detroit?"

"I am embarrassed to say it, but Father Charles E. Coughlin, an ordained priest, was in the Moon, wearing a straight suit—I mean, no Roman collar—shooting craps and fondly patting the fanny of a hard-looking little blonde."

"Are you sure it was he?"

"I know the man well. He saw me and winked. He knew I wouldn't tell on him."

"You must have fascinating stories about the Silver Moon. But let's return to Andrea Alphand."

"I spoke to Sarge. He spoke to me. He didn't offer to introduce his companion of the evening. A couple of days later I ran into him in a bar. I asked him who

the redhead was. He told me. He said her name was Andrea Alphand and he was glad to have broken up with Jessica, which had made it possible for him to begin seeing Andrea. He said she was French and a journalist."

"Have you ever seen her since?"

"Never."

"It is possible—not likely perhaps but distinctly possible—that she killed Sargent Peavy, Vito Francione, and Charles Flaherty."

Once more, Kennedy was silent for a moment. "Beverly Hill," he said.

"Can you describe her more thoroughly?"

"I only saw her for a moment. Her red hair captures your attention. Then . . . dark eyes, a pug nose, pouty lips, a gorgeous figure. Altogether, a memorable woman."

"Dark eyes? Brown eyes? With red hair?"

"I guess that's a little unusual."

"Yes, Mr. Kennedy, that's unusual."

"My God! You think Sarge had on his arm that night the hitter hired to kill him?"

"It is not impossible. Having dropped Jessica Dee, he made a suspiciously quick transition to this Andrea Alphand. Suppose she came here, flaunted herself, gave him exotic and apparently enthusiastic sex, and—"

"I get the picture," said Kennedy. "And it's not impossible. Sarge was susceptible."

"Do you know anything more about the woman?"

"That's it. I saw her once. I spoke with him about her once. He was filled with enthusiasm, called her *perfect*. A man who would give up Jessica Dee and then find another woman perfect had to have been mightily impressed."

Mrs. Roosevelt owned a blue Buick that she had bought in 1933, and she enjoyed driving herself, though the Secret Service insisted that an agent accompany her when she went out. This morning Stanlislaw Szczygiel was available. Though an agent of his seniority did not ordinarily simply ride with the First Lady when she went out for a drive, he went with her this morning because she was driving to the campus of George Washington University to meet with Letitia Peavy.

Professor Peavy sat in a typical professorial office: happily cluttered with books and papers. The occupant of this professorial office looked anything but professorial, with her marcelled hair, bee-sting lips, stylish black silk dress, and commanding bustline. Mrs. Roosevelt wondered what her students thought of her.

"Let me introduce Mr. Stanislaw Szczygiel. He is a senior agent of the Secret Service and has done some

investigating into the murder of Mr. Peavy."

Letitia nodded solemnly. "There has been no progress, has there?" she asked. She gestured toward two straight wooden chairs, the ones used no doubt by students who came in for conferences with her.

"I should not be quite that pessimistic," said Mrs. Roosevelt as she sat down.

"Jessica Dee killed my husband," said Letitia bluntly. "I can't see why anyone would have a moment's doubt of that."

Mrs. Roosevelt smiled faintly, tolerantly. "Do you think she also killed Charles Flaherty and Vito Francione?" she asked.

"What's that got to do with anything?"

"All three were killed with the same nine-millimeter pistol," said Mrs. Roosevelt. "We know for an absolute certainty where Miss Dee was at the time when Mr. Flaherty was killed. She was nowhere near the Mayflower Hotel."

"Flaherty . . ." said Letitia. "A sleazy, vulgar man. I always regretted Professor Peavy's accepting a directorship at the Cabot National Bank of Boston. Charlie Flaherty was . . . Well, no man deserves to be murdered, I suppose."

"You are aware, of course, that some of the officers and directors of the bank are under investigation and may become the subject of criminal charges."

"That does not surprise me. The professor often

came home with tales of horror about loans the bank made with insufficient collateral. He always opposed such loans."

"Mr. Szczygiel has discovered exactly that, in the course of his inquiries," said Mrs. Roosevelt.

"Professor Peavy had faults we all are painfully aware of," said Letitia, "but he was scrupulously honest in the way he conducted himself as director of several banks—and as a member of the Federal Reserve Board."

"I have heard nothing whatever that contradicts a word of that," said Szczygiel.

"Thank you."

"Allow me to change the subject," said Mrs. Roosevelt. "Tell me, do you enjoy The Thayer?"

"Thayer . . . ?"

"The Hotel Thayer, at West Point."

"Oh— Oh, yes. The professor and I attended an economic conference there two or three years ago. It's fine hotel. I enjoyed it."

"Was that the only time you stayed there?"

Letitia nodded. "The only time."

"I was there last Friday. Someone I met said he had seen you in the hotel that morning. Obviously he was mistaken."

"Mistaken, yes."

Mrs. Roosevelt smiled. "All of which has nothing to do with why I came to see you this morning." She

changed her smile to a frown. "There is reason to believe that Mr. Peavy was murdered by a hired professional killer. There is reason to suspect that the murderer—of Mr. Peavy, Mr. Flaherty, and Mr. Francione, all three—may have been a woman. I recalled that you told me two weeks ago that you saw Mr. Peavy having lunch with a red-haired woman. It is not impossible that the hired killer is a red-haired woman. Can you give a fuller description of her?"

Letitia shook her head. "He told me that she was a secretary at the Fed. I saw nothing about her that might have denied it. As I recall, she had on a blue dress, not very expensive—something from Sears maybe. She was attractive, I suppose. Maybe that dress clung to her a little more than modesty would have dictated. I didn't pay much attention to her, and when the professor said she was just a secretary, I saw no reason to think otherwise. Are you suggesting she . . . ? He . . . ?"

"She may have replaced Jessica in his affections," Mrs. Roosevelt said sympathetically.

"Which," said Letitia indignantly, "does not explain Jessica's earring in my bedroom!"

"Ye pay me too much honor," said Jessica on the telephone to Mrs. Roosevelt.

"Well, you seemed to enjoy last evening's cocktail hour so much that I thought it appropriate to invite

you to visit me late this afternoon and stay a few minutes longer for the President's 'at home.' "

"I shall be there."

The First Lady hung up the phone. Hick was there with her in her study. She knew Hick would want to go to the cocktail hour, so she herself would have to go, and Jessica would be a charming addition. Her real reason for inviting Jessica was something entirely different. She wanted to ask her a question or two.

When Jessica appeared in Mrs. Roosevelt's study, she was wearing a perky powder-blue beret and a flower-print cotton dress with a frilly white collar. Her skirt was unstylishly short for that year, barely covering her knees, and crept back and *uncovered* her knees when she sat.

The First Lady was always a little envious of women who chose their clothes well and wore them well—two things she could not do. She had been comfortable and attractive in the simple, soft-lined dresses that were the style when she was a young woman. From the time when skirts became narrower and shorter, the dictates of fashion had victimized her. All but invariably, she wore too much ornamentation. The simple classic lines of her inaugural ball gown had flattered her; almost everything else she wore damaged her image.

She watched Jessica settle gracefully into a chair and smooth her dress with one quick flip of her hand.

"I may say to you," Mrs. Roosevelt told her, "that you are *almost* absolved in the murder of Sargent Peavy. It would still go well with you if you would tell us whom you were with the night he was killed, also where you were the night when Vito Francione was killed."

Jessica smiled gently. "I am sorry, Ma'am," she said.

"Very well . . . for now. But I do recall something and want you to amplify on what you said. You told Lieutenant Kennelly that Mr. Peavy was seeing another woman already at the time of his death. You told Lieutenant Kennelly that woman was a 'spectacular redhead'—the words he quoted you as saying. Is that true? Was Mr. Peavy seeing a redheaded woman?"

"Yes."

"Since you describe her as a spectacular redhead, may I assume you saw her?"

Jessica nodded. "Yes, I did. You remember that Sargie gave me a pair of earrings not very long before he died—"

"One of which was found—"

"Yes. On the bedroom floor, beside his body. Well . . . He bought those earrings for me at Duncan's, on Eye Street. I formed a sort of habit of looking in when I walked past Duncan's. The place was a good memory for me—until Sargie was murdered and one of the earrings was lookin' to put a noose around me neck."

"Were you in Duncan's with Mr. Peavy on the day when he bought the earrings?" Mrs. Roosevelt asked, remembering that Letitia had said Peavy brought the earrings home and showed them to her before he gave them to Jessica.

"Noo. We were in the store one day. I saw those earrings and admired them, nivver dreamin' Sargie would buy them for me."

"Alright. The redhead . . . ?"

"I looked in Duncan's one day, and there the two of them were—Sargie and a red-haired wooman. Spectacular was the word for that one! It looked like he was buyin' *her* a gift."

"If you saw her again, would you recognize her?"

"Well . . . maybe. I saw her mostly from behind."

"Then what led you to the conclusion that Mr. Peavy was buying her a gift?"

"Wull . . . Pattin' her on the behind, he was. And when he stopped doing that, he held her hand. Cozy."

"Brother John," said President Roosevelt, extending his hand across his desk. It amused him to call J. Edgar Hoover by his first name. Hoover didn't like it much but had never indicated so. "And Brother Clyde," the President added, shaking hands also with Hoover's devoted sidekick, Clyde Tolson. "Welcome to both of you."

The director of the FBI and his second-in-

command took chairs at the sides of the President's desk in the Oval Office.

"We appreciate your time, Mr. President," said Hoover smoothly.

The director—the title by which he insisted he be called by all FBI personnel—was forty years old and didn't look quite that old; there was a childlike innocence about him in total contradiction of his iron-fisted administration of the Federal Bureau of Investigation. He and Tolson visited Atlantic City from time to time, where they took snapshots of each other with a simple Kodak, like a pair of boys playing on the boardwalk. He also liked to play the horses and to eat with Tolson in Washington restaurants, where he never paid the check.

"What can I do for you?" the President asked.

"Perhaps I can do something for you, Sir," said Hoover. "As you ordered, I have remained away from the investigation into the murder of Sargent Peavy—though I cannot but confess I think we would have made more progress than has been made in the past two weeks. Which is neither here nor there."

"Yes," the President agreed. "Neither here nor there."

"I am, however, in possession of a piece of information I think you and Mrs. Roosevelt may find interesting."

"Go ahead."

"I am sure, Mr. President, that you have heard the name Isabel Rosario Cooper."

"Refresh my memory," said the President.

"Last year, General Douglas MacArthur sued the columnist Drew Pearson for $1,750,000, claiming that Pearson had libeled him in columns describing his conduct at the time of the Bonus March. The suit was abruptly withdrawn when Pearson's lawyers announced they would be calling Isabel Rosario Cooper as a witness."

Tolson grinned broadly as he listened to this.

"We at the Bureau already knew about Isabel," Hoover continued. "When the Chief of Staff, United States Army, is keeping a mistress in a hotel suite, that is a matter of national security."

President Roosevelt shrugged. "My attitude was, so what? General MacArthur is unmarried and can keep a woman if he wants to."

"Not if you are Douglas MacArthur," said Hoover. "The big, bold general is a mama's boy. He couldn't bear to have it known that he was sleeping with a Eurasian woman."

"Which has to do with what?" the President asked.

"The chief of staff, being a naughty boy, I thought we had better keep an eye on his affairs. Well . . . he has another girlfriend. General MacArthur has had for some time an amorous relationship with Mrs. Sargent Peavy. He takes her up to West Point from time to time

and shares with her a suite in The Thayer."

"Is it your impression, Brother John, that Sargent Peavy knew about this?"

"I don't know."

"Did you know about Peavy's affairs?"

"With Clare Boothe? Oh, yes."

"Jessica Dee?"

Hoover nodded. "Jessica Dee."

"Andrea Alphand?"

"I never heard that name," said Hoover.

"A redhead, variously described as striking, spectacular, and so on."

"No. Have no information on her."

The President laughed as he reported to Mrs. Roosevelt about his conversation with J. Edgar Hoover.

"The man has an ear for scandal," she said. "Which shouldn't surprise us. We knew that."

While Jessica and Hick joined the President for his cocktail hour, Mrs. Roosevelt met briefly with Ed Kennelly and Stan Szczygiel. "I suppose, she said, "we have to eliminate Mrs. Peavy's lover as a possible suspect. It is hardly likely, I should think, that General Douglas MacArthur killed Mr. Peavy."

Kennelly scratched his chin. "I suppose not," he said. "Still . . . Still I wonder if we can learn where the general was on the evening of February twelfth."

•   •   •

The First Lady stopped by the President's cocktail hour for a moment, to take Hick away for their evening. They meant to have dinner and then to attend a performance of two one-act plays by Clifford Odets. The first of these was *Till the Day I Die*. which was a powerful anti-Nazi protest. The second was *Waiting for Lefty*, a play about the New York City taxi strike. Mrs. Roosevelt was determined to see the play, and to be seen seeing the play, because it had been closed in Boston and members of the cast arrested on charges of obscenity and blasphemy. It had also been closed by the law in New Haven and Philadelphia.

The evening promised to be challenging.

The President wanted anything but a challenging evening. After he had bathed and had been assisted into bed, Missy came down from her suite, wearing a nightgown and peignoir as usual. They ate their dinners from trays, then settled down to watch a movie.

The Bell & Howell company had made a gift to the President of a sixteen-millimeter sound projector, and some of the Hollywood studios sent him sixteen-millimeter versions of their pictures. Missy had learned to thread and run the projector, and tonight she mounted a big reel—the first of several—and focused the show on a big portable screen that had been earlier set up by the valet. The movie was *Mutiny on*

the Bounty, starring Clark Gable and Charles Laughton.

The President and Missy reclined against heaps of pillows and settled down to be entertained.

XIII

ED KENNELLY SHUFFLED THROUGH a stack of reports. That was half his job: looking through endless memoranda and reports. He was impatient with them, as always. By chance, maybe, one caught his eye. He had asked for a copy of any report of a woman with a gunshot wound. And here was a report of a wounded woman—

GUNSHOT WOUND REPORT

Rcvd: 2/24/35
From: Dr. Jacob Goldish, 1118 Eye St.

Miss Darlene Givens, 1130 H Street, age estimated 30–35 yrs. appeared today morning to receive treatment slightly infected gunshot wound on right hip. Stated that brother had accidentally discharged rifle while cleaning it, bullet

had grazed subject's hip, and subject had not taken matter seriously until symptoms of infection appeared. Treated subject by cleaning and dis-infecting wound. Urged her to return in two days.

Kennelly drove to 1130 H Street. The subject had given Dr. Goldish a false address—as in fact did half the reported gunshot-wound victims who visited doc-tors and hospitals. Dr. Goldish, though, was real, and Kennelly interviewed him.

The doctor was a no-nonsense man with a long, strong jaw, a flushed complexion, and retreating yellow-blond hair.

"Red hair? No, Sir. Miss Givens had curly dark hair, cut very short. I'd call her an exceptionally attractive young woman. Cute little nose with some freckles on it. Dark eyes. And . . . Well, to speak frankly, yet trying to be circumspect, she had an unforgettable figure. I have to say, she was the kind of young woman who makes even an old doctor sit up and take notice. I've seen   "

"How old was the wound, Doctor?"

"I'd say almost a week. It hadn't been terribly se-rious to begin with and had been healing nicely, but a minor infection had developed, and she was well ad-vised to come and see me."

"Would you guess the shot was fired at her from behind or from the front?"

"It would be extremely difficult to say. It was in the soft, fleshy part of her buttock and had come nowhere near her pelvis."

"I assume she had no other wounds."

"None that she showed me."

"Can you add anything more to your description? How was she dressed?"

"Interesting," said the doctor. "She had a muskrat fur coat with a fox fur collar. Very distinguished. Very expensive. But when she took it off she was wearing a plain white middy blouse and a gray pleated skirt, like a schoolgirl. Then . . . her stockings were silk, nothing cheap about them. And she had to take down her . . . Well, she was wearing step-ins, not bloomers. Silk. A strange ensemble, I thought."

"What you estimate as her age?"

"Thirty, I should guess. She's no little girl."

"How would you react if I tell you she may have committed three murders in Washington this month?"

"I would say I think that's impossible."

"Would you recognize her if you saw her again?"

The doctor grinned. "Well . . . most of the time she was here she lay on her stomach on my table with her skirt up and her step-ins down. My attention was given to her backside, and even so I would not recognize that. But, seriously, I think I would recognize her face. She is no forgettable young woman."

Kennelly showed the doctor a photograph of Blaze

Flame. The doctor laughed and said, "No, Sir. I've seen her recently. She's got no bullet wound on her butt."

Kennelly sat down with the First Lady in her study. Stan Szczygiel was there.

"I have to concede," he said, "that Jessica Dee is pretty well out of it. So is Blaze Flame. So is Letitia Peavy. We are left with Andrea Alphand."

"Unless it was a man," said Szczygiel.

"Which doesn't explain why Peavy was naked and had experienced a sexual orgasm within the past hour," said Kennelly.

"You overlook a possibility," said Szczygiel grimly.

"*Sargent Peavy?*" asked Mrs. Roosevelt.

"Why not?

"That would open up an entire new set of possibilities."

"Worse than that," said Kennelly. "It would put us all the way back to square one."

"I can think of but one possible source of information," said the First Lady. "Letitia Peavy."

"I can think of but one person who could ask her," said Kennelly.

If Letitia were to be queried on this subject, it seemed appropriate that it should be over a quiet private luncheon in the White House. When Mrs. Roosevelt gingerly broached the question of whether or not Sar-

gent Peavy might possibly have had a homosexual relationship, Letitia guffawed.

"*Sarge?* I was married to the man for seventeen years! He had his quirks alright, but that wasn't one of them!"

Mrs. Roosevelt nodded. "We are running out of suspects."

"Find a burglar," said Letitia.

"A burglar?"

"A burglar. If no one can accept the idea that Jessica's earring proves she was present when Sarge was murdered, then someone must have broken into her apartment and stole it. Find a burglar."

"Could that have been Mr. Francione's role?" Mrs. Roosevelt asked Kennelly on the telephone. "He was, after all, a legbreaker. Maybe he was more."

"Brought down from Boston to burglarize Jessica's apartment and steal the earring so the murderer could plant it in Peavy's bedroom? That seems more than a little fanciful to me."

"I suppose so. Will you be distributing a new description of the suspect to your men?"

"Better than that," said Kennelly. "I sent a sketch artist to visit Dr. Goldish. Together they produced a likeness."

"Then may I offer a suggestion? I suggest you have that sketch reproduced and shown to ticket agents at

the railroad station, also at the bus stations, even at the airline ticket counters. If 'Andrea Alphand' has finished her work here, she may be leaving the city. Indeed, I am afraid she has already left."

That Thursday evening Mrs. Roosevelt spoke to the people gathered for a dinner of the American Youth Congress. The AYC was generally friendly, but not entirely friendly, to FDR and the New Deal. Many of its members felt that the President was not doing enough for young people, and they demanded he do more.

Mrs. Roosevelt said to the assembled delegates and their guests—

"I was amused the other morning by a newspaper headline that referred to my husband's philosophy as a 'mollycoddle' philosophy. The accompanying column contrasted Franklin Roosevelt unfavorably with Theodore Roosevelt, stressing how strenuous and active a life Theodore lived and how sedentary and easy Franklin's life is.

"Well . . . My friends, I need hardly remind you that I have known both men on a familiar basis. I respectfully suggest to you that any man who has brought himself back from what might have been a life of invalidism, to become a model of physical, mental, and spiritual strength, can never honestly be called the devotee of a 'mollycoddle' philosophy.

"I visited not long ago a small town in West Virginia

where a mine disaster had claimed the lives of a dozen miners. I met a young widow, pregnant and with two small children, whose husband was one of those miners. They had just decided to try to buy the small house they rented, so as to own a home of their own. Now that young woman will receive thirty dollars a month from workmen's compensation. If we had Social Security, which Congress has not yet enacted into law, she would get twenty-seven dollars more. I ask you. Is the President trying to 'mollycoddle' this young widow by proposing that we pay her an additional twenty-seven dollars?"

Arriving back at the White House, the First Lady discovered on her desk a note—

Call Lt. Kennelly, any hour.

She placed the call to police headquarters, and Kennelly came on the line.

"Bingo!" he exulted. "I've got the little cutie with the bullet-wounded butt. You were right. She was getting ready to absquatulate. Your suggestion that we watch the railroad station and so on was absolutely right. She was buying a ticket on the Orange Blossom Special to Miami and would have been out of here tomorrow."

"Who is she?"

"We've sent her fingerprints to the FBI and will have a report in the morning."

"How nearly satisfied are you that she is our woman?"

"She was carrying a small pistol in her purse, not the murder weapon but a deadly little twenty-five caliber automatic. She had almost a thousand dollars in cash on her, plus the keys to a rental car."

"Rental car?" Renting automobiles was a very new thing, and Mrs. Roosevelt had to be impressed with the resourcefulness of a young woman who could rent a car. She understood that renters had to deposit a cash bond with the rental companies, in the amount of several hundred dollars. "She *rented* a car?"

"Yes, Ma'am. A Chevrolet. Anyway, she's a beautiful woman. There's more excitement in seeing her clothed than in seeing Blaze Flame naked. And she's tough. She takes the attitude that her arrest is a funny joke. She says we're all gonna be embarrassed tomorrow, 'cause we've got nothin' on her. She's lying on her back in a cell, smoking a cigarette, and showing no sign of being uncomfortable or scared."

"I shall want to see her."

"Of course. But let's wait until tomorrow morning, after she's had a night locked up and has maybe started thinking of something. Besides, in the morning we'll know if the FBI has a fingerprint record of her."

•   •   •

"Her name is Carol Tupper," said Kennelly. "She's from California. Did six years in the slammer out there for assault and battery with a deadly weapon."

Carol Tupper was chained to a chair with two pairs of handcuffs, one locking each wrist to a chair arm. Kennelly had said to Mrs. Roosevelt that he regarded this young woman as dangerous; probably she was the notorious hit woman Beverly Hill. He had explained also that she had not been changed into a jail uniform. She had refused to wear one and said she would be naked in her cell if necessary; and they had decided it was not worth a fight to try to force her. That she was a beautiful young woman was beyond question. Her oval face was flawless. Her dark eyes captured first attention, then her cute button of a nose with a few freckles. She did not need lipstick to improve the shape of her mouth. She was wearing a white middy blouse with blue sailor collar, with a pleated gray skirt. If her figure had not been extravagant, she might have had the girlish gamine look she apparently tried to affect.

"Mrs. . . . *Roosevelt?*" she muttered, eyes wide. "What have you got to do with this?"

The First Lady settled into a chair facing her. She smiled at Carol Tupper. "I am personally interested in the death of Mr. Sargent Peavy," she said.

Carol Tupper shook her head. "They say you can

show up anywhere. Planning on attending my hanging?"

"Are they going to hang you, dear?"

Carol glanced at Kennelly. "What *he's* got in mind,"
she said. "Could you have him let me have one hand
loose so I can smoke a cigarette?"

"You'll have plenty of time to smoke," said Kennelly. "Anyway, Mrs. Roosevelt doesn't like to have to
breathe cigarette smoke."

"I can't even scratch my nose."

Kennelly pulled out a handkerchief and rubbed the
tip of her nose.

"Thanks," said Carol sarcastically.

"You've been cuffed before," said Kennelly.

She nodded. "Which makes you think you've got
me by the short hairs. Once a person has a record—"

"And lies," said Kennelly.

"Anybody who's ever been roughed up by the cops
learns to lie to them."

"You haven't been roughed up."

"Not here. Not yet. But it's coming. I've gone
through it before. Fire hose. Cold water. Naked. Pretty
soon you say whatever they want you to say. Then off
to the slammer and a record that sticks to you for the
rest of your life."

"Suppose I assure you," said Mrs. Roosevelt, "that
nothing of the kind is going to happen. Lieutenant Kennelly will give me his personal assurance."

Kennelly nodded. "No fire hoses. No beating. No nothing. All we want is some straight answers to straight questions. Why did you give us a false name when we arrested you?"

"Simple enough. You got a criminal record, you're in big trouble, no matter what. I hoped you wouldn't find out who I was."

"Why were you carrying a concealed weapon?"

She smiled slyly. "Looka me. Guys grab me. Guys try— I got so I carry my little gun, for protection."

"How'd you get the gunshot wound on your butt?"

"It's not a gunshot wound. I was crossing the street. A car with a flapping fender damned near ran me down. The fender cut me."

"You told Dr. Goldish it was a gunshot wound."

"If he figured I was cut by a rusty fender, he'd want to give me tetanus shots. Ever have one? Thank you, no more. Talk about pain! So I told him my brother shot me, and he cleaned and dressed the wound. I knew he'd file a report, so I didn't give my right name and address. I didn't want to talk to the cops." She tugged on her handcuffs. "I knew it would wind up like this."

"I'm going to mention three names," said Kennelly. "You tell me if you knew any of these men. Charles Flaherty."

Carol shook her head. "The name means nothing to me."

"Vito Francione, also known as Frankie One."

"Never heard of him."

"Sargent Peavy."

"I don't know any Sergeant Peavy, or Corporal Peavy, or Private Peavy."

Mrs. Roosevelt thought she detected a diminution of the young woman's confidence as she heard these names. The change was subtle but detectable. She exchanged a glance with Ed Kennelly. He had noticed it, too.

"You bought a ticket on the Orange Blossom Special," said Kennelly. "How come?"

"I'm a California girl. I wanted to get where there's some sunshine. Wanted to go on the beach."

"How long have you been in Washington?"

"Since Monday."

"Why'd you come here?"

"To see if I could find a job. I came east to see if I could find a job. I heard the government was hiring girls for office work, so—"

"Can you type, take shorthand?"

"You bet I can! Good, too. The State of California taught me, while I was doing my time."

"Where did you apply for a job?"

"I didn't. I decided I didn't like it here. It's too cold."

"That's a nice muskrat coat you were wearing

when you were arrested. You saying an office girl can afford that?"

"A guy gave it to me. Guys give me things sometimes."

"You should've taken the label out of it."

"What you mean?"

"A label sewed inside one of the pockets says it belongs to a Mrs. Wilbur Sackett of Philadelphia. She reported its theft to the Philly police and is going to be mighty glad to get it back."

"Hey! I didn't lift that coat. Maybe the guy who gave it to me did, but I didn't, for damned sure."

Kennelly shook his head. "Odd," he said. "A girl like you . . . I figure you're pretty smart, but you aren't smart enough to keep sticky fingers off a fur coat."

"A guy gave it to me, I tell you!"

"Not smart," said Kennelly with regret Mrs. Roosevelt could almost believe was genuine.

Kennelly sent Carol Tupper back to her cell.

"We know one thing for sure," he said. "Her real name *is* Carol Tupper. At least, that's the name she did time under, in California. The fingerprint match is perfect." He glanced at his watch. "I want to put in a call to California. They should be up by now out there."

He picked up his telephone and told an operator he wanted to talk to someone in the detectives' office,

Los Angeles Police Department. He hung up while they waited for the call to go through.

"I can't believe she would have been so stupid as to steal that coat," said Kennelly to Mrs. Roosevelt.

"Maybe she didn't."

"True. Maybe she didn't."

"If you will forgive me, Ed, I shall go to the bath-room."

"You know where it is," he said, adding with a small grin. "You've been here often enough."

When she returned, the call to California was being connected. Kennelly handed her a small extra earpiece wired to his candlestick telephone, so she could hear both ends of the conversation.

"This is Lieutenant Edward Kennelly, District of Columbia Police, Washington," Kennelly said loudly.

"Sergeant Bill Dickerson, Los Angeles PD. What can I do for you, Lieutenant?"

"We have in custody a young woman named Carol Tupper, of Los Angeles, on suspicion of murder. The FDI fingerprint record says she spent time in prison out there, for assault and battery with a deadly weapon. We'd like to know what you can tell us about her. Also, we understand there's a professional killer in Los Angeles who goes by the name Beverly Hill. We—"

"That'd be Captain DeLong's file. Let me see if I can get him."

Kennelly and Mrs. Roosevelt waited. Then—

"Captain Lucian DeLong here. "You say you're in Washington?"

"Right. Washington, D.C."

"And you've heard the name Beverly Hill?"

"Right. The woman I've got in custody is named Carol Tupper. I wonder if they could be the same person."

"Tupper. Right," said Captain DeLong. "I'll send for that file. So far as Beverly Hill is concerned, she may be a fairy tale. We keep hearing the name, but we don't know anything about her. The story is that she's a beautiful woman who hires out to kill men. I'll believe it when I see it."

"Do you know anything about Carol Tupper?"

"I will when I get the file."

"What about Beverly Hill?"

"The story is told that she's a dangerous hitter who's knocked off . . . The numbers vary. Some say as many as a dozen men. But no one has ever seen her. If she's real, she's clever."

"Our killer seems to be a crack shot with a pistol."

"We— Okay, here's the Tupper file. What's the gal you got in custody look like."

"Bee-*yoo*-tiful!" said Kennelly.

"I'm looking at her mug shots," said the captain. "Taken in 1926. She was twenty-one years old at the time. Beautiful? She sure was. She's the kind of girl

you hate to lock up; it seems like such a waste. Okay, she did six years on a charge of assault and battery with a deadly weapon. The deadly weapon was a pistol. Her victim was a beer baron. She got him in the leg, then damned near got killed herself when his boys opened fire on her. She ran. She fired a couple of shots at the guys who were shooting at her. They hit the sidewalk, and she got away. The beer baron didn't want to prosecute, but our boys talked him into it. He could identify her. He knew who she was. So she went to the crowbar hotel. She's a parole violator, incidentally. We'll put a hold on her. We'll bring her back out here if you don't make your case against her."

Mrs. Roosevelt gestured to her hair.

"What did her hair look like?" Kennelly asked.

"Dark and curly. I can't tell from the picture if it was marcelled or is naturally curly. But . . . dark and curly."

"Anything more?"

"Her mother was a hooker, and her father was a pimp. Daddy is dead now. When she gets back to the slammer, she can say hello to Mommy, who lives there, doing a five-year for mugging a John."

"We'll hold her for you," said Kennelly. "But I'm beginning to believe she's going to be staying here more or less permanently."

XIV

"YOU KNOW," MRS. ROOSEVELT said thoughtfully to Ed Kennelly, "I can almost feel sorry for that young woman. If she is not convicted of murder here, she is going back to California to complete her sentence, or she is going to Philadelphia to answer for the theft of a muskrat coat."

"We have to face a fact, Ma'am," said Kennelly. "The young woman is a tramp."

Mrs. Roosevelt nodded. "We must wonder what she might have become if she had come from a normal family background."

"Well . . . In the circumstances, we have to hold her."

"I am sure you do. I . . . You know, Ed, Jessica says she saw Sargent Peavy in a jewelry store, apparently buying a gift for a young woman. That store is Duncan's, on Eye Street. It might be well to check."

• • •

Kennelly checked. Yes, Mr. Sargent Peavy had been in
the store and had purchased a gold butterfly pin set
with rubies. Since he was a member of the Federal
Reserve Board, the store had accepted his check. In
fact, it had accepted his check before, when he bought
a pair of earrings. Shown the mug shot of Carol Tupper, the clerk could not be sure. The face did look
familiar, but the woman with Mr. Peavy when he
bought the pin had had long red hair.

That afternoon—it was Friday—Mrs. Roosevelt did
the kind of "Hawkshawing" the President emphatically wished she would not do. She accompanied Ed
Kennelly and Stan Szczygiel on a search of Carol Tupper's rooming-house room.

She insisted Kennelly must get a search warrant.
Accompanying a police officer on an authorized
search was one thing. Breaking and entering would be
quite another.

They arrived at the address in a marked police patrol car, driven by a uniformed officer. Kennelly wore
his badge conspicuously outside his jacket. Szczygiel
wore the badge of a Secret Service Agent. The First
Lady wore a Secret Service badge on her dark-blue
dress. She hoped the veil on her hat would sufficiently
obscure her face that she would not be recognized.

The boardinghouse was run by a Mrs. Lunal, a
spare, angular, gray woman who wore round steel-

rimmed spectacles and volunteered as the first words after their introduction that she was a "widder woman" who had to work too hard.

"I struggle, and I have to watch my pennies too, y' know, to put a decent meal on the table. But them boarders, they jus' gobble it down without hardly stopping to taste anything. They never say of anything, 'That's good. That there's tasty, Miz Lunal.' But let one of them find fault with somethin', I hear about it. 'This here succotash is too salty, Miz Lunal. This here succotash needs salt, Miz Lunal.' Tupper? That gal hardly ever eats a meal here. She's hardly ever here for supper. 'Course, that means she pays fer what she don't git, so I s'pose I shouldn't complain. The Swiss steak she don't eat winds up ground into the next night's stew, along with her share of the succotash."

"How long has she lived here?" Kennelly asked.

"Her? Moved in the week before Christmas. I'll be frank to tell ya, I don't think she's a good girl. I suspicion she's— Well . . . I won't say it. She wears a fur coat, rides in cabs. I think there's somethin' wrong with her."

"We'll search her room," said Kennelly.

Mrs. Lunal shrugged. "Yer the cops. You suspicion she's a whore? That what ya think?"

"No, that's not what we think."

"Well, not outa my boardin'house she ain't. I prom-

ise ya that. I keep a respectable establishment. There's no such goin's on here."

Carol Tupper's room was the best that could be found in a modest, respectable boardinghouse. It was furnished with a brass bed, a plush easy chair, a small table with a straight chair, and a bureau. It had a closet, where a woman's clothes hung.

"The advantage," said Kennelly, "is that you have to check in at a hotel, which puts your name on a record. Carol Tupper could stay in this boardinghouse six months, pay her rent with cash, and depart, leaving no record she was ever here."

"And if she made no trouble, a woman like Mrs. Lupal would soon forget her," Mrs. Roosevelt suggested.

"Precisely," said Kennelly. "Another reason to suspect she's a pro."

The First Lady stood aside while Kennelly and Szczygiel searched the room. She had a profound sense that, no matter what Carol Tupper was charged with, this was a painful invasion of her privacy.

The two men went through her clothes, checking in pockets, feeling for anything that might be sewn into a lining. They turned over her mattress and there found a small crowbar—a burglar tool. They went through her underwear and stockings in the bureau drawers. In the top drawer of the bureau they found a

gold butterfly studded with rubies: the very pin the clerk at Duncan's had described.

But no pistol.

Stymied, the two men stood in the center of the room and looked around. Szczygiel turned over the rug.

Mrs. Roosevelt stared at the bureau. "Excuse me," she said. "You are the detectives, but I seem to recall reading somewhere—in a work of fiction, I believe— about something being taped to the bottom of a drawer. I wonder if it would be wise to look at the bottoms of the drawers."

Kennelly moved immediately to pull out the top drawers. He found nothing taped to the bottom of the left-hand drawer, but taped to the bottom of the middle drawer was a key.

Letters and numbers were stamped on the bow of the key—

F & M N B
335 LG
COLLEGE PARK

"It's a key to a safety-deposit box," said Kennelly. "Farmers and Mechanics National Bank, College Park, Maryland."

• • •

Kennelly and Szczygiel obtained a warrant from a federal magistrate, and at 4:45 in the afternoon they appeared, with Mrs. Roosevelt still lightly disguised, at the Farmers & Mechanics National Bank of College Park.

Farmers & Mechanics was a small-town bank. When a Secret Service agent, a D.C. police lieutenant, and a D.C. policewoman presented the warrant, the president himself hurried out to the banking floor.

"My name is James Gritty," he said. He was a short man with thick white hair and a flushed face, wet eyes, and full lips that tended to flutter. "I suppose, strictly speaking, I should ask our lawyer to check this warrant. On the other hand—" He shrugged. "We're not talking about a big depositor." He blinked over the warrant. "Box 335 Lg. That means large box. Let's go see who it belongs to."

He led them inside the bank's vault, where a bank gnome had a detailed card record of the box. "That box belongs to Mrs. Edna Taylor," he said. "Rented five years in advance."

Kennelly used the key from Carol Tupper's apartment and Gritty used the bank's key to take the box out of the wall. It was a large box, the largest the bank offered. Gritty put the box on a shelf in a cubicle and left to allow the three to examine the contents. He left with them, too, the card that showed the dates on which Carol Tupper had visited the box.

The first item that caught their eye was a luxuriant red wig.

"There you have it!" Kennelly bawled. "The answer!"

Mrs. Roosevelt ran a hand over the smooth, natural human hair of what had to be a fantastically expensive full wig. "I should think it answers a great deal," she said quietly. "But what else have we. What an ugly pistol!"

Kennelly covered his fingers with a handkerchief as he lifted the pistol from the box and laid it on the shelf. "What we expected," he said. "This is a Beretta Model 1934. That's the silencer. It's a pro's weapon if ever I saw one. We'll take this straight to the ballistics lab and fire it into a box of sawdust. The slugs will match the ones found in Peavy, Francione, and Flaherty. If they don't, I'll chew one up and swallow it. We got our lady."

Also in the box was $10,000 in cash and a tiny notebook containing telephone numbers.

"Look at these dates," said Mrs. Roosevelt, pointing at the bank's card record. "The box was rented on December 27, 1934. She opened it on February twelfth and thirteenth February nineteenth and twentieth and twice on February twenty-sixth once in the morning and once in the afternoon."

Szczygiel ticked off the dates on his fingers. "She took the Beretta from the box on February twelfth,

shot Peavy with it that evening, and returned it to the box the next day. She took it out on February nineteenth, killed Francione with it that night, and returned it the next day. She took it out on the morning of the twenty-sixth, killed Flaherty with it, and put it back that same afternoon."

"For her," said Mrs. Roosevelt, "everything depended on her not being identified with this box. It might have lain here for years, unnoticed—a box belonging to a Mrs. Edna Taylor."

The Beretta, fired into sawdust for a ballistics test, proved to be the murder weapon in the three murders. It was, however, entirely free of fingerprints.

The wig— Well, it explained much, but how was it to be clearly identified with Carol Tupper? Wigs did not take fingerprints.

The telephone company responded immediately to a request from the Secret Service and identified two of the numbers from the notebook as the telephones of the executive offices of the Cabot National Bank of Boston and the residential number of Charles Flaherty.

Returning to her study in the White House, Mrs. Roosevelt received this information by telephone. She found herself in a condition she rarely experienced: tired. She was happy to sit down at her desk and sip

e tea Tommy had brought her, look at the afternoon
wspapers, and put aside for the moment the calls
it had accumulated while she had been out "Hawk-
wing." Indeed, she was so tired that she decided
: would indulge in a pleasure the President often
enjoyed in early evening: a hot bath.

She sat in the water, no newspapers at hand, no
letters, no memoranda, soaped herself only lightly,
and just luxuriated in the comforting water. She remembered her years in England, when visiting the
"baths" was what Society did. Thank God, this Washington tap water did not stink of sulphur or whatever
minerals made the baths of Europe so salubrious. She
wished Hick were still there and that they had a bathtub big enough to share. William Howard Taft's enor-
mous tub had long since been removed. It would have
accommodated two people easily.

"Ma'am . . ."

"Tommy."

"Mr. Kennedy is on the line. He seems to think
what he has to say is important."

She did not like to talk on the telephone in the
bathtub. It seemed somehow indecent, as if her caller
could be aware that she was stark naked. But Mr. Kennedy had been helpful, and she nodded to Tommy to
carry the telephone, at the end of its twenty-five-foot
cord, into the bathroom.

"I understand it is not a convenient time for you

to receive a telephone call, but I thought you would like to know that Terrence Corcoran has arrived in Washington."

"Corcoran?"

"Terrence Corcoran is president of Cabot National Bank of Boston. He has come down by airplane to arrange for the shipment of Charles Flaherty's body.

"By airplane?"

"Yes, Ma'am. All the way from Boston."

"Thoughtful of him."

"Well . . . maybe. He would very much appreciate an opportunity to meet with you."

"We are on the verge of solving the mysteries of the deaths of Mr. Peavy, Mr. Francione, and Mr. Flaherty. On the *verge*, Mr. Kennedy."

"Could you give Terrence fifteen minutes?"

"I cannot refuse to talk to someone who may have something to say that I should hear."

"May I bring him to the White House, say in the next half hour?"

She swished her hand around in the water around her. It was no longer hot. "Very well, Mr. Kennedy."

The Boston banker was no very great surprise. The Boston Irish—Fitzgeralds, Kennedys, Murphys, Curleys, O'This's, and O'Thats—were of a certain sameness: often red-or sandy-haired, burly, blustering, and, as the cliché went, men who had fervently kissed the Blarney Stone. They could charm— Well, the bromide

was, the spots off a leopard. In point of fact, they couldn't. The leopards knew them too well.

"I never supposed," said Terrence, "I would ever have the honor of *entering* th' White House, much less of being received by the First Lady."

"Blarney, Mr. Corcoran," said Mrs. Roosevelt, not using the term exactly correctly but so that he understood what she meant.

Terrence Corcoran grinned. "I knew I was going to meet a formidable woman."

"I imagine Mr. Kennedy would rather be sitting with the President at his cocktail hour," she said. "Since it is that hour, I have ordered gin and vermouth, and Scotch, to be brought up. With ice. You will have to pour your own. I am not skilled at mixing cocktails."

"Very gracious of you," said Kennedy.

"I understand you've come to take home the body of Mr. Flaherty," she said to Corcoran. "As Mr. Kennedy may have told you, I believe we are on the verge of solving the mystery."

"I'm afraid," said Corcoran, "the solution will do nothing for the reputation of poor Charles Flaherty. I'm afraid it won't do much for several of us, including me."

"I think you had better tell Mrs. Roosevelt the whole story," said Joseph Kennedy.

Corcoran nodded. "Our fathers founded the Cabot National Bank of Boston and gave it the name Cabot

as a way of cocking a snoot at the Boston Brahmins. It was *our* bank, our thing, y' know. Nobody's money was in it but *our* money."

"He means Irish money," said Joe Kennedy. "All the depositors were . . . friends. Maybe forty or fifty families."

"We set up the bank to help each other in business," said Corcoran. "If one of us needed money, Cabot Bank would lend it."

"Often with insufficient collateral," said Mrs. Roosevelt dryly.

"We'd take care of each other if necessary. If a loan went bad, the rest of us would cover it. It was a cozy arrangement. The problem was—"

"The problem was," Kennedy interrupted, "that they got greedy. Other depositors came along, meaning depositors who weren't party to the cozy arrangement. By the by, Cabot National Bank was lending *other people's money.*"

"And losing some of it," said Corcoran dolefully. "But it was okay until . . . until banks began to fail."

"And Cabot failed," said Kennedy.

Corcoran went on. "We figured that, given time and patience, we could straighten everything out and nobody would lose money. But some people didn't have patience, and we didn't have time. There was a run on the bank, depositors demanded money we didn't have, and the bank had to fold."

"It was a hell of a way to run a bank," said Kennedy.

"Absent the Depression, we would have prospered."

"Absent what rabbits do at breakneck speed, there wouldn't be so many rabbits," said Kennedy.

"And Sargent Peavy?" asked Mrs. Roosevelt.

"He was an ornament," said Corcoran. "We put him on the board of directors to make the bank look respectable. We always had two or three of those."

"And he consistently voted against your extending loans to people with insufficient collateral," said Mrs. Roosevelt.

"Which was fine," said Corcoran. "We didn't expect him to do otherwise. But . . . When the examiners came around, when the bank failed, we had to realize that Peavy would be called as a witness. He would be asked to testify as to *why* he voted no on all those loans."

"And Sarge being Sarge," said Kennedy, "he would have testified exactly why."

"Which might have sent some of us to prison," said Corcoran. "One vice president has left the country. He lives in a cottage in Ireland, in much reduced circumstances."

"So the rest of you decided to kill Mr. Peavy," said Mrs. Roosevelt sternly.

"No! No!"

A steward from the kitchen arrived with the Scotch and gin and vermouth. He hadn't been told to bring a martini shaker, so Kennedy mixed two martinis on the rocks, in the glasses. Mrs. Roosevelt accepted a splash of Scotch over ice.

Corcoran was shaken, but he accepted the drink Kennedy mixed for him and took a big swallow to start. "Nobody decided to kill Sargent Peavy. We talked about ways that we could use to discredit his testimony. We even talked about bribing him. But nobody talked about killing him."

"Are you prepared to deny that none of you had anything to do with his death?" the First Lady asked.

"Well . . . I can only give you the facts. Early in January, Charles Flaherty said to the rest of us, 'Give me $25,000, and I'll see to it that Sargent Peavy doesn't testify against us.' As God is my witness, Mrs. Roosevelt, I believed he meant he would bribe him."

"And?"

"We gave him half the money. He disappeared. We wondered if he hadn't taken the $12,500 and skipped the country. But he reappeared.

He said half the money had helped but that we couldn't be sure of everything until we came up with the remaining $12,500."

"Which you gave him?"

"Which we gave him. Once again, he disappeared. But we were more confident that time. Then we learned of his murder. He's dead, and the $25,000 is missing!"

XV

THE FIRST LADY FELT certain she knew almost the whole story now, but she would rely on a favorite, and classic, technique to confirm what she thought and fill in gaps. At eleven o'clock on the morning of Saturday, March 2, 1945, a group she had summoned met in the Cabinet Room, in the East Wing of the White House, only one room removed from the Oval Office.

The President stopped in for a moment as the group was assembling, to greet them briefly and jocularly wish them well in their Hawkshawing. Though he was jaunty, he knew this was an entirely serious meeting with probably ominous results.

Mrs. Roosevelt would preside over the meeting, from the head of the table. At the far end, opposite her, sat Louis McHenry Howe, assiduously dragging on a Sweet Caporal. That he was there was evidence of how seriously the President took this meeting—so seriously in fact that he did not think it politically wise

to be there himself. To Mrs. Roosevelt's left sat Stanlislaw Szczygiel, and beside him was Jessica Dee, colorfully dressed in a pink sweater and white skirt, then Joseph Kennedy, and the Boston banker Terrence Corcoran. Of the four chairs to the First Lady's right, three remained vacant. The fourth chair on the right side of the table was occupied by Letitia Peavy, stiff and brittle, if not hostile, and wearing a royal-blue dress.

A stenographer sat at a small table, with a stenotype machine, ready to take a record of everything that was said.

A large and floridly ornate coffee urn—a White House heirloom from the days of President Grant—sat on a sideboard, with a smaller pot of tea and a tray of little pastries. Everyone had a cup of coffee or tea and a pastry or two on a plate.

"Ye have no br-rought me here to slip the noose around me nick, have ye?" Jessica said very quietly to Mrs. Roosevelt, with a sly grin.

"No, dear. I believe you have been spared. Of course, we must hear what the witnesses have to say."

"Tha' one," Jessica said, shooting an unfriendly glance at Letitia, "still believes *I* did it."

"You return the favor," said Mrs. Roosevelt. "You think *she* did it."

"Noo," said Jessica. "I think the rid-hid did it."

"We shall see," said the First Lady. She turned and for a moment stared thoughtfully at a group of card-

board cartons that sat on a table. "We shall see."

The door from the corridor opened, and a uniformed police matron entered the Cabinet Room. She glanced around as though to satisfy herself that no one ominous was present, then reached back and pulled Carol Tupper into the room by a heavy chain that circled the prisoner's waist. Ed Kennelly followed, taking Carol's arm and leading her to a chair at the table.

Kennelly sat to Mrs. Roosevelt's right. Carol sat next, between Kennelly and the matron, who took the chair next to Letitia.

The participants in the meeting sat thus—

Mrs. Roosevelt

Kennelly	Szczygiel
Carol	Jessica
Matron	Kennedy
Letitia	Corcoran

Howe

Stenographer

Carol Tupper had some days since been persuaded to submit to the uniform of the District jail and sat glumly in a loose dress of blue-and-white-striped tick-

ing. She was tightly restrained by the chain around her middle, to which was attached at each side a single handcuff, pinning her hands to her hips. She could barely move, and Mrs. Roosevelt wondered—but refrained from asking—if it were really necessary to curb the prisoner so cruelly.

"We have coffee, tea, and some pastries," she said. She nodded at the matron and added, "Perhaps you could assist Miss Tupper with something."

Jessica joined Kennelly and the matron in carrying three cups of coffee and three plates of sweets to the table. The matron carefully put a cup of coffee to Carol's lips and let her sip.

"Thank you," Carol muttered, not without a trace of sarcasm.

Mrs. Roosevelt opened the meeting, signaling to the stenographer that she should now begin taking a record.

"I shall be happy to hear the suggestions of others, now and throughout our meeting, but I think it wise to begin by advising Miss Tupper that she has certain rights. Mr. Howe, will you advise her?"

Howe's cigarette wobbled between his lips as he said, "This is part of the ongoing investigation into the murders of Mr. Sargent Peavy, Mr. Vito Francione, and Mr. Charles Flaherty—of which crimes, Miss Tupper, you are suspected. You should understand, then, that

whatever you say here will be taken down and may be used as evidence against you. Do you understand?"

Many years would pass before some such a warning would be required by decisions of the Supreme Court of the United States, but it seemed to the First Lady that decency required it, and she had asked Howe to give it.

"Now . . ." she went on. "The first question we should address, as it seems to me, is that of identification. We have in the room three witnesses who believe they saw Miss Tupper in the company of Mr. Peavy. Do you continue to deny, Miss Tupper, that you ever met Mr. Sargent Peavy?"

"I never met anybody by that name."

Mrs. Roosevelt spoke to Letitia. "Mrs. Peavy. Is this the woman you saw having lunch with your husband?"

Letitia raised her chin and stared at Carol. Her slow nod clearly suggested she was not sure.

"Well . . ." said Mrs. Roosevelt. "Lieutenant Kennelly, let's see if we cannot facilitate the identification."

Ed rose from his chair and went to the table where the cartons stood. He opened one and pulled out the red wig.

Carol blanched. She shook her head violently, trying to prevent the detective from settling the wig on her head. She struggled against her chain. The matron

grabbed her by the nose and held her head still while Ed settled the wig on her head.

Letitia pointed at Carol. "Yes. She's the one I saw having lunch with Sarge. At Allegro."

Carol's face was now flushed with anger. She tossed her head and tried to throw off the wig. "Allegro!" she yelled. "I've only been in that place once in my life. I had lunch there with Fred Logan."

Ed Kennelly opened a file and held up before Carol a photograph of Sargent Peavy. "Fred Logan?" he asked.

She nodded emphatically. "Fred Logan."

"Miss Dee," he said. "Do *you* recognize this woman?"

"Yes," said Jessica softly. "I saw him with her in Duncan's Jewelers, on Eye Street. I didn't get a very good look at her, but I'm pretty sure."

Kennelly opened another carton and took out the butterfly pin. "Did Fred Logan give you that, Miss Tupper?"

Carol stiffened, and her cheeks flushed even redder. "That . . . *Where did you get that?*"

"Where do you suppose? Did Fred Logan give you that pin?"

"Yes. He and I were . . . pretty good friends?"

"*Were* good friends? Where is he now?"

"I haven't seen him for a coupla weeks. He went on a business trip. To Kentucky. He's in coal."

"When he bought you this pin, did you notice that he paid for it by writing a check in the name Sargent Peavy?"

"No, I didn't notice how he paid for it."

Ed nodded at the First Lady, and she nodded at Joe Kennedy.

"I saw Sargent Peavy and this woman together in a Virginia roadhouse called the Silver Moon. They were being quite chummy."

"Not as chummy as you and *that* one," Carol snarled, nodding toward Jessica. "*Two* chummy couples. You two are in cahoots!"

"Three witnesses saw you in the company of Sargent Peavy," said Kennelly.

"No, they didn't. They saw me in the company of Fred Logan. Anyway, what's it prove?"

"I'm afraid it proves a great deal, Miss Tupper," said Mrs. Roosevelt gently. "You know where we found the wig. You have to know what else we found there."

Ed Kennelly opened still another carton and lifted out the 1934 Model Beretta.

Carol Tupper's jaw trembled, and tears began to streak her cheeks.

"It has been fired into a box of sawdust, and the slugs were compared to those taken from the bodies of Mr. Peavy, Mr. Francione, and Mr. Flaherty. It is the pistol used to kill all three of them. Have you any ex-

planation as to why it was in *your* safety-deposit box?"

Carol wept. She lowered her chin to her chest and shook with sobs. After a minute or so, she looked around the table and said, "You . . . got me. I knew it . . . would happen sometime. *I knew it!*"

"Take this wig off me and let me have a hand loose so I can drink a cup of coffee, and I'll tell you the whole story. Why not? What difference is it going to make to me now?"

Ed Kennelly pulled off the wig, exposing once more her tight, curly, dark hair, and the matron freed Carol's right hand.

"You don't know 'bout people like me. You don't *care* 'bout people like me. I was born to be locked up in a cage, like an animal, which I've been, and to drop through a trapdoor with a rope around my neck, which I will be. Didn't take a depression to make *me* poor. I was dirt poor from the day I was born. But—" She lifted her chin high. "But I've known the best this life offers: champagne and caviar, suites in the best hotels, rides in roomettes on the best trains . . . I've even *flown* across the country. How? 'Cause I'm good at what I do. I'm the *best!*" She shrugged. " 'Course, I always knew how it would end. I always knew. Well . . . Rather drop to the end of a rope than to live the life I'd have had to live otherwise."

"You dramatize," said Louis Howe.

"You've chosen your way of dying," she said, glaring at him. "You're sucking your death into your lungs this very moment. I chose my way. So . . . You want to know the story?"

"We do," said Mrs. Roosevelt.

Carol Tupper lifted the fresh cup of coffee the matron had brought her, sipped, and took a pastry from the plate. "The last decent food I'm ever going to eat," she said bitterly.

Mrs. Roosevelt turned to Ed Kennelly. "I believe Lieutenant Kennelly will see to it that you are fed decently," she said.

Ed nodded. "If she tells the story."

Carol sighed. "I don't know what good it does me to tell you the story, except maybe that. How 'bout treating me decent for the time I've got left? I mean, smokes, decent food, newspapers and stuff."

"Good enough," said Kennelly.

"Then, where do you want to start? Yeah, I'm Beverly Hill. What difference? You've got me on three counts. That's enough. Okay. I came to Washington to kill Peavy. Not the other two. I wasn't surprised when I had to do the other two, but it wasn't part of the deal."

"Charlie Flaherty—" said Corcoran.

She interrupted. "He came to Los Angeles and offered me $25,000 to kill Sargent Peavy. Hell. I'd have taken a contract to kill the Pope for twenty-five grand.

It was my retirement. On top of what I had, that would have retired me. I knew it would be dangerous. He was a high government officer, in a city I didn't know. I'd killed guys from a distance, some up close . . . What difference does it make if I tell you that Peavy was number thirteen? Unlucky."

"He gave you $12,500 in advance," said Corcoran.

"Exactly. So I came to Washington, got myself a room, rented my deposit box, rented a car, and set to work." She paused and stared for a quick moment at Letitia. "Peavy was no problem. He'd just broken off with—" She looked at Jessica. "—*that one* and so was desperate for a new connection. I trailed him for a few days, made occasion to meet him, and—Well, you can imagine. Imagine something else. Imagine the night in a hotel bedroom when I took off the wig!"

"You wore the wig when you were at work, so to speak," said Ed Kennelly.

She nodded. "And sometimes when I took it off it was the sexiest thing a guy ever saw. Anyway . . . It wasn't difficult to set up a thing with Sarge. He liked to run his hand over these little short curls and tell me the damndest things. He told me all about his marriage, all about *that one*. He told me about the sapphire earrings he'd bought her and how that purchase had almost busted up his marriage."

"And you decided to steal my earrings and—" Jessica interrupted.

"Steal *one* of your earrings, dear," said Carol. "A person's born poor like me is nothing if she doesn't know how to break into an apartment. Sure. I got into your place and took one of the sapphire earrings. I figured—what the hell?—I might as well try to lay the murder on somebody else."

"You are an evil woman," Letitia said, scornful to the utmost.

"As are you, Ma'am," said Carol. "Need we go into the reasons why Sarge needed relationships with a chippy like *that one* and a pro like me?"

Howe had kept quiet for the most part. Now he spoke. "So you shot Sargent Peavy right between the eyes. Damned good shooting, it has been noted."

"If you commit yourself to my line of work," she said, "you learn to use the tools of your trade."

"And to choose them," said Kennelly. "That Beretta is one of the finest pistols made in the world today."

"Y'll hang me, I won't tell you the name of the gunsmith who made the silencer," Carol said defiantly.

"Honor among—" Howe started to say.

"There *is* such a thing," she interrupted him.

"You entered the Peavy home," said Mrs. Roosevelt. "You—"

"I had a key. He'd given me a key. I did what I had to do to dull his suspicions, if he had any, and then—"

"Are we to understand that you confess you shot

and killed Mr. Sargent Peavy?" asked the First Lady.

"For $25,000, half in advance, half when the job was done." Carol shrugged. "I'd deny it if you didn't have me cold. The way it is . . . What the hell?"

"We found rubber gloves at the Peavy place and in the hotel room," said Kennelly.

She nodded. "And you didn't find any fingerprints on the Beretta," said Carol.

"When you shot Francione?"

"Lovely kid gloves."

"Alright. Who called the police and reported the death of Peavy?"

"I did. From a telephone booth."

"Why?"

Carol turned toward Letitia. "Soft-hearted Sue. I thought it would be better if the cops found the body than if Mrs. P found it. Could I have some more coffee?"

Jessica took the cup from the matron and poured coffee for Carol.

"There is a great deal more to the story," said Mrs. Roosevelt.

Carol received the coffee from Jessica's hands. "Sorry I had to try to make it look like *you* did it, kid," she said. "I didn't know you from Adam, and it was a good idea for me to try to make it look like *somebody* else did it."

Jessica smiled at her, half sweetly, half bitterly. "I

had what they call an ironclad alibi," she said.

"And didn't have to use it. I wish *I* had an ironclad alibi."

"Noo. I din't have to use it. Bu' it was there."

"You got your second $12,500," said Mrs. Roosevelt to Carol. "From Mr. Flaherty's hotel room."

Carol Tupper nodded. "I got most of it. He'd handed $2,500 to a man he'd hired to kill me. He didn't intend to pay me." She sipped coffee. "He'd got the money from his partners, and he meant to keep it. He's not the first man to hire me and try to cheat me out of my fee. Well . . . When you try to make a living doing what I was doing, you don't dare let the word get around that you can be diddled. When they try that on you, you have an obligation to yourself."

"I figure he had another reason," said Kennelly.

"Right. I was a threat to him. I never did blackmail a client, but he didn't know that. Even if I didn't try that, he'd have been in big trouble if the cops got me. I'd sing to save myself. He knew that."

"So—"

"Flaherty was a dead man from the moment he hired Frankie One to kill me. The deal was, Flaherty was to hand me my second $12,500 when he saw newspaper stories about Peavy's death. I went to see him at the Mayflower—wearing my own hair—and he told me the money had not come down from Boston yet but he'd have it in a few days. He told me to call him

in a couple days. I should have killed him then and there and lammed with the money, which was in his suite just the way I figured. But I was wearing my own hair and might have been identified. I figured I'd go along with him a little while."

"Tell us about Frankie One," said Kennelly.

"I was coming to that. When I called Flaherty again he asked me to meet him at the Blue Diamond on K Street. I went there. He wasn't there. I didn't figure he would be. What was there instead was Frankie One. I didn't know who he was until I read his name in the papers, but I had him figured: a guy Flaherty had hired to do me in. He tried to put the make on me. It didn't take me a minute to see through him. Okay. In a way Flaherty had done me a favor. If his hit man winds up dead in the alley behind K Street, he'll pay quick. He'll see how Beverly Hill does business."

Mrs. Roosevelt was sickened by this cold recitation and faced it with grim resolve. So was Letitia, who turned her back to the table and covered her face with her hands. Corcoran, the banker, stared, open-mouthed, and drew deep breaths. Kennedy focused on his hands where they lay on the table. Jessica glowered at the confessing hit woman, more curious than appalled.

"The second time I saw him, Frankie invited me to go with him to a good French restaurant, saying his car was parked out back. I said no. In the dark alley

where he said his car was parked, he'd shoot me or stab me. I knew he would. I was sure he would. I called Flaherty, and he promised to be at the Blue Diamond on Tuesday night—this being one week after I'd killed Peavy for him. I knew he wouldn't show. I knew Frankie *would*. This time he changed his story. He said he was Flaherty's driver and that Flaherty was waiting for me at Coq au Vin. His car was out back."

Carol Tupper paused and allowed her face to distort with a devilish smile. "Flaherty hadn't told the cheap little legbreaker what he was facing—I mean, facing a pro. I doubt he even told the jerk I was a hitter. I knew he'd try to kill me in that alley. And he did." She shook her head, still smiling a malevolent smile. "Flaherty hadn't warned him he was up against a pro. I had the Beretta in a cheap purse, and I didn't even pull it out; I just blew the end out of the purse."

"But he shot you, too," said Mrs. Roosevelt.

"I should have put one through his eyes, just to make sure. When I was walking away, he managed to get his pistol up and graze me on the hip. That's a bad thing when you're in my line of work. You don't dare show the wound to a doctor. Eventually I had to."

Ed Kennelly shook his head skeptically. "You shot Frankie on the nineteenth and Flaherty on the twenty-sixth, a whole week later. What was going on that whole week?"

"I know what was going on with me. I can guess

what was going on with Flaherty. Me, I was lying on my belly in bed, nursing a butt ripped across by a thirty-eight slug. I poured alcohol on it, and I bandaged it, but I couldn't very well walk. I limped. Just when I thought it was getting all better, I saw the red streaks coming off it. That's when I went to see Dr. Goldish, which I suppose I should have done the first day."

"But why didn't Flaherty go back to Boston?"

"My guess is that he was trying to find somebody to do what Frankie had failed to do."

"How'd he know you hadn't gone back to California?"

"Because I called him at the Mayflower and told him I wanted my money."

"Did you tell him you'd killed Frankie?"

"I didn't want to say anything like that on the phone. He knew."

Except for Ed Kennelly, Carol Tupper's statement was giving the people around the table a glimpse into a world they had hardly known existed. Gangster movies were popular, and they had all seen them, but none of them had seen or heard anything like this young woman's calm recitation of what she obviously regarded as the simple facts of a simple story.

"Are there many like you?" Louis Howe asked her.

Carol smiled at him. More accurately maybe, she sneered. "I give you credit, old fellow. You and the President are trying to change what makes people like

me. But don't imagine there are just a few of us."

"Women?" Mrs. Roosevelt asked quietly.

"I'd rather be a hitter than a hooker," said Carol bitterly. "You're going to hang me. I know that. Okay. I'd rather hang than live poor. And there's thousands that would—including, yes Ma'am, women. I might have made it; I mean, made it to a kind of retirement, maybe a nice little cottage in Florida. I had a chance. So I took it. I've got just one regret: that I got caught."

The matron fastened Carol Tupper's cuff on her right wrist again and led her from the Cabinet Room. In the doorway she turned and showed an almost-appealing smile.

The room was silent for a long moment.

Mrs. Roosevelt broke that silence. "Mrs. Peavy," she said, "you caused us a moment's concern about you when you said your husband was killed as you were driving from the university to your home. We had to wonder how you knew that."

Letitia shook her head. "I guessed," she admitted. "It seemed like it had to be."

"Very well. I want you to know that the Director of the FBI knows who your paramour is. I cannot and do not blame you for lying to me about The Thayer. I suppose most women would. But you should tell your friend the Director knows. He is not a man in whose discretion any of us can place much confidence."

"Yes," said Ed Kennelly. "And one more question in the privacy and confidence of this room. Don't ask me how I know, but— Mr. Kennedy, Miss Dee, you seem to be seriously concerned about certain photographs. Do you want to suggest why they are of so much concern?"

Kennedy flushed deeply. "I . . . I . . ."

"*I'll* answer yer question, Leftenant," said Jessica. "Fer our a-*mews*-ment, I allowed Mr. Kennedy to photograph me in the nee-wed. Noo, we wou'nt want sich photographs to be seen by ithers, wou' we? Of course, it was wi' *him* I was the night when poor Sargie was shot."

Joe Kennedy's embarrassment would have generated laughter at the end of any but the distressing meeting now closing.

"Mrs. Roosevelt . . ." he said.

"None of us here traffic in gossip, Mr. Kennedy," she said.

XVI

CAROL TUPPER OFFERED NO spirited defense when she was tried for murder. She was convicted and sentenced to death by hanging.

The sentence was carried out at noon on Tuesday, May 7, 1935, on a gallows erected in the Navy Yard, where the District performed its occasional execution. Lieutenant Ed Kennelly was present. He reported to Mrs. Roosevelt when the grisly procedure was finished but did not tell her any details.

Carol was not jaunty as she mounted the steps of the gallows, but neither was she tearful. As she had suggested in the meeting in the Cabinet Room and said more specifically to the chaplain who accompanied her, death was but a part of life, and she had chosen a way of life that had made it likely she would not live to an old age.

As she stood on the trapdoor, the executioner did what he had explained to her he would do in her cell

half an hour before. He tied a rope around her waist, to which was attached a hundred-pound bag of sand. The extra weight, he said, falling with her to the end of the hanging rope, would make sure that she died immediately of a violently broken neck and would not have to hang and kick and strangle.

For her last scene, she wore her red wig.

On September 8, 1935, Senator Huey Long was assassinated in the Louisiana State Capitol in Baton Rouge. Left without a job and with notoriety surrounding her that would deny her other employment, Jessica Dee suggested to Joe Kennedy that he support her. Kennedy took over the rent on her Washington apartment, where he visited her at least twice a week and paid her a monthly stipend. This arrangement continued until February of 1938, when Kennedy sailed for London to take up his duties as United States Ambassador to the Court of St. James. Rose Kennedy, then recovering from an appendectomy, was unable to sail with him; but Jessica did, and he established her in a flat in Kensington. In time she met and was taken under the wing of Brendan Bracken, the wealthy English adventurer who suggested openly that he was the illegitimate son of Winston Churchill. Bracken established a trust fund for her and bought her a house in Wimbledon.

When General Douglas MacArthur's term as Chief

of Staff, United States Army, expired, he accepted an appointment to command the armed forces of the Philippines. Letitia did not accompany him. On the voyage there, he met his future wife. Letitia returned to Harvard and in 1939 married a fellow professor.

Terrence Corcoran was one of four officers of the Cabot Bank who was sentenced to prison. He served two years in the Massachusetts State Penitentiary. The others served three and four years.

Blaze Flame became a featured performer at the 1940 World's Fair in New York, where she danced completely nude behind a huge balloon that she artfully manipulated to conceal and reveal herself under pink lights.

Mrs. Roosevelt saw her performance when she visited the Fair. The dancer learned the First Lady had been in her audience and sent her an autographed photo, signed with the name she was then using—

The balloon is handsomer than the handcuffs, don't you think?

Hope Charity

Also by Elliott Roosevelt

MURDER
IN
GEORGETOWN